Milk and Honey

Milk and Honey

a novel

ELIZABETH JOLLEY

Persea Books / New York

First published in Australia by Fremantle Arts Centre Press in 1985.
First published in the United States of America by Persea Books in 1986.

For information, contact the publisher:

    Persea Books, Inc.
    225 Lafayette Street
    New York, New York 10012

Library of Congress Cataloging-in-Publication Data

Jolley, Elizabeth, 1923–
    Milk and honey.

    1. Title.
[PR9619.3.J68M49   1986]   823   86-4896
ISBN 0-89255-102-X
ISBN 0-89255-103-8 (pbk.)

This book is offered as an expression of thanks to Ian Templeman. He has not only provided me with publishing opportunities with Fremantle Arts Centre Press but, as Director of the Fremantle Arts Centre, invited me ten years ago to conduct classes in the art of writing and the enjoyment of literature at the Centre and through its outreach programme, Arts Access, the chance to meet a great many people and to see places I would never otherwise have visited. Thanks are due to the people who, over the years, have come to my classes or expressed the wish for me to visit their towns, their farms and their homes.

    I thank also the Western Australian Arts Council, The Literature Board of the Australian Council and express gratitude to Ray Coffey, Managing Editor of Fremantle Arts Centre Press. It is a privilege for me to be a small part in the history of Fremantle Arts Centre Press since its inception in 1975.

Elizabeth Jolley, June 1984.

Love seeketh not itself to please,
Nor for itself hath any care,
But for another gives its ease,
And builds a Heaven in Hell's despair.

Love seeketh only self to please,
To bind another to its delight,
Joys in another's loss of ease,
And builds a Hell in Heaven's despite.

Songs of Experience, William Blake

... and to bring them up out of that land unto a good land
and a large, unto a land flowing with milk and honey...

Exodus ch 3. v 8.

Milk and Honey

A wind blew through Europe. It blew stronger and ever stronger. It swept up the soot and the dirt, the horse manure, the brickdust and the thistledown.

Countless whirlwinds, spiralling and gathering, carried all that which was not fixed and secure upwards into the sky. And in this twisting movement cones were formed which, because of the intensity of the whirlwind, grew more and more compact as they moved higher and higher into the winds above the firmament.

The clotted debris travelled far away into another hemisphere and, forgetting the winds, sank down to earth. Most of the cones, as they reached the earth, fell apart and mixed with the dust of the new place.

Some did not do this.

Even as they fell they pressed closer and closer into themselves as if this was their only means of surviving.

In the new land they were scattered like rocks, not mixing with the soil but, from time to time, settling on the fragments of other such cones from which they drew sustenance in order to preserve themselves and remain unchanged for as long as possible.

I

This was the street where Madge, suddenly worried that she had forgotten her tampax, drove slowly, unconcernedly, taking up the whole road while she fumbled mysteriously to find out.

'I'll have to tell him something,' she said, 'what'll I tell him? He is my husband after all. What'll I tell him Jacky? What'll I tell him?'

In this street I seemed always to be hearing Madge, her voice and her laughter like an echo singing, extending from a hidden corner in my mind to the tops of the trees and along the lonely telegraph wires. It was hard to believe that there had been a time when I had not known her beyond those overheard conversations during rehearsals, disjointed sentences, in hoarse whispers, half hidden behind the flaps of music.

Later I experienced in the seclusion of her car, in the warm scent given off from women's clothing and soft leather upholstery, made fragrant by her sitting on it, an excitement in the possibility of knowing her more. She created an atmosphere of intimacy and tenderness which was out of reach and yet was offered. It was like seeing the hint of the colour of petals in an unopened bud. There was always the promise of something more. This promise was sweet and wonderful and I waited for my happiness delicately.

'I'll have to tell him something. What'll I tell him Jacky?' It was as though her voice still whispered like a ghost in the street.

Every day I ached with loneliness. There was no Madge and no music. When I drove into the street in the mornings, I wished that the woman sitting in the car further down the street could be Madge. Knowing it could not be her, knowing that one person cannot replace another, I started every day with my sad wish.

I could not stand being a door to door salesman. Every morning I sat in the car in the street which was the first street on the way out to the hut; I had no energy to start selling. Madge's hut was the place where we went on Thursdays. On Thursdays, though it was her husband's living, Madge took the car. She went to the hairdresser early and then drove with me to the lonely hut where, on the deserted shore of the estuary, we could have some hours alone together.

The street which had once been the way out towards my happiness became one of the boundaries of my territory, my selling area. It was a suburb between the railway line and the sea, a place of closed houses and loneliness.

Every morning I sat in the car unwilling to start out with the ugly squat cases which were packed with hair spray, deodorants, furniture cream, toothbrushes, jellies and free samples of shampoo and face cream.

'I'll take the free sample then,' the housewives said, attempting kindness, glad to have something for nothing. Every sample cost me five cents but I could not say so. Later on I stopped giving the free samples.

'The worst form of self-abuse, 'Madge would have said, 'to use your own free samples.'

My wife said nothing about them at all, only snipped off a corner of the blue foil and smoothed the cold cream round her tired eyes. Her hands were rough from housework and from her work in the factory where she repacked damaged soap cartons, starting every morning at seven thirty. She used up a sample a night, her hands seeming to need and absorb unlimited grease.

'Nutmeg graters!' Madge would have held up her own puffy hands, laughing even as she was complaining. My wife never thought of things like that to say. She never laughed and she never complained. She hardly spoke at all. Sometimes I heard her chide Elise softly as she hurried the little creature in the mornings, hustling her round to a neighbour whose house was as shabby as our own. The neighbour looked after Elise till my wife came up the hill from the factory at half past four.

My work depended entirely on my own energy. Some days after repeated failure I had no energy. I could not face the bruise of being unwanted at doors. Often all the doors were closed; no one came to answer my knocking. On these days I went home early and was there before my wife came in. I sat alone in the narrow kitchen staring at the chill discomfort of poverty, wishing that she would come home quickly to light the stove and, with her presence, silent as it was, clear away the misery.

Sometimes I tried to enjoy walking from house to house in the calm, clean air. I tried to stop thinking of things as they were and I listened to the contented conversation of the doves. Endlessly they talked to and fro. From one house to the next the voices of the doves accompanied me. And, on some mornings my head reeled with the silvery liquid music of the magpies.

I left calendars stamped with my name and address at all the houses up one street and down the next. No one sent for me wanting a long list of things. Sometimes I sold

3

something, a jar of prepared mustard, a deodorant powder, two or three items in a morning. I seemed to feel hungry very quickly and I sat eating, without satisfaction, in a derelict corner shop. I longed for real coffee. I trembled with the longing for real coffee. I thought of the Beach Hotel where, if I ordered coffee, it would be easy to spend all I earned.

The hotel had a luxuriousness which I knew did not really exist. The ugly concrete and the troublesome drains were poorly disguised with red carpet, gilded mirrors and the blue washed hair of the receptionist. In spite of the braided uniform of the lift boy and the heavy cutlery in the dining-room, I knew it to be a place where people took a room for an afternoon.

It was easy to think of the locked door, the brief inspection of the Rules on the back of the door, the laughter on testing the springs of the bed and the solemn moment when laughter changes to undressing. So nearly had we attempted this ourselves, but seeing too quickly through the moment of urgency the dreary ending, Madge said, 'It's no good! I can't sink so low!'

We walked on, passing the dark opening into the hallway, with its mixed smells of kitchen mistakes and spilled wine fermenting, wishing for a place where we could be close together in love, secretly.

No Madge and no music, for I could not play my cello now with my damaged hand. The skin had healed and drawn my fingers into a kind of claw. I was able to drive the car and I could just carry the case. I kept the hand hidden in a grey cotton glove as it was badly discoloured. I could not look at my hand without remembering the terrible scene and the unexpressed agony in Tante Rosa's severe face as she stood with the curtains blazing all round her. She did not utter a sound then, but later moaned ceaselessly in her pain as she lay with blackened cloth burned into her body. Heloise and Louise, not daring send for a strange doctor, tried to look after her and to attend to me using remedies they knew, sitting up all night till there was nothing they could do beside

4

Tante Rosa, except sit there while she died.

Every day now I kept asking myself the same thing. Why had Madge come to the house at all that afternoon?

My damaged hand was always cold and it ached. Somehow I associated the ache with the cold little house we now had. It was on a steep hill in front of the factories. Immediately behind was a stagnant pool of greenish water, factory waste; it seeped away to the river behind. From the narrow verandah in front of our house we could look across other similar houses, crazily packed one above the other, on the steep little roads which led down to a small shipyard and a harbour and on to the sea.

It could have been a pretty place with charm but for us it became at once the embodiment of failure and suffering. My wife looked and was unhappy. She kept herself and the child scrupulously clean and she worked long hours. Her body seemed withered with work. We did not see our neighbours. I left the house later than my wife. Most of our neighbours had left too by the time I eased my shabby car and its load of cosmetics and household things off the narrow piece of wasteland at the side of the house. No one from the street ever asked to buy from me; I never expected them to, but I would have been pleased if they had.

Norman came to dinner on Sundays; his white hair showed like a bandage under the brim of his hat. He was, in a sense, my benefactor. Help came to me from where it could be least expected. Norman helped me at the time of the disaster into the business in which he had been for years, successful in the kind of success which depended entirely on his own personal effort. Should this fail then there was nothing to sustain him. He allowed his own business to falter while he gave up time to come with me. Together we sold my expensive car and he took me to buy a second-hand one and he showed me how to set about finding a cheap house to rent, and then he suggested I start in the same business. He told me what products to buy first and he taught me about the products and how to sell them.

It seemed to me that everything was made from clay. We depended entirely upon the earth. Earth, this clay from which the body is nourished and, in all forms, is applied to the body; the fine golden clay of face powder, the coarser clay of poultices and rouges and creams and lotions. It is as though the body springs from the earth and needs the earth in order to live and then, in the end, is returned to the earth to be buried deep in clay. Sometimes I longed for that burial. How could I speak of this to my customers and how could I speak of this to Norman and my wife?

I liked my products, I liked the clean smell in the car. They were all good things. Lovingly I cleaned the bottles and packets with my handkerchief. I wrapped up the foodstuffs in plastic and always kept a piece of old curtain folded over the boxes to keep everything as clean as possible.

'Keep your display cases nice,' Norman said, 'fresh things always. People buy through their eyes,' and he made little telescopes out of his hands and held them to his eyes.

Sometimes I sang softly as I knocked on doors nestling in seedy concrete where woody sticks of hibiscus, without flowers, poked in through the broken louvres on the side verandahs. I waited hopefully while a dog barked in the emptiness beyond.

'If only we had some friends,' I said to my wife one evening.

'Why ever?' she said without looking up.

'To get them to buy something,' I said, my mind heavy with bottles and packets unsold. I went to sleep every night with them all weighing on me and woke as if handling them, as if showing them to a prospective customer already.

'If we had any friends, they wouldn't buy,' she said bitterly, 'friends would hold back from buying, they would think you were making money off them.' She sighed. I knew she was right. She had not spoken so much for days. Bitterness. I was glad all the same, to hear her say something.

Sometimes in the evenings she sang in her soft voice, alone in the bedroom, producing the s softly as they all did when they spoke their Viennese German together. Even Tante Rosa, despising Madge, did not sound too harsh in the music and the softness of these sounds. When I heard my wife singing some small song sadly I wept, turning my face away from the door so that, if she came in, she would not see my tears. I wept for the comfortable household, for those things of that household which made it comfortable, for Leopold who had once seemed so loving and kind, for Tante Rosa and her pain and for Aunt Heloise who later sat, embarrassed, on plastic covered pillows in the Sunset Ward of the District hospital, waiting for a letter or a visitor.

Sometimes, after my cup of real coffee in the Beach Hotel, I sat outside on the small, sandy cliffs looking down on to the sea as it came up in long, slow waves to the rocks and sank sighing back down the beach and I felt the profound melancholy that all my life has come over me from time to time. It was the melancholy of dark trees standing alone and the quiet sadness of the colours of the land, dark greens and browns and the sand subdued. As I sat, the colours deepened, tawny, dun coloured blending beneath the low grey sky. And from somewhere hidden, the sun lit up the sea.

This same melancholy was mine after loving Madge, when I was exposed, stripped, sad in the relaxation after desire. It came to me too in the long sustained notes of the cello, the second movement of the Haydn cello concerto; always when I played this something wept inside me. I felt it when the big house was dark and hushed, years ago, at the time of Louise's illness, it was relieved only by the excitement and happiness of knowing Madge more and more.

And the mulberry tree which had been Waldemar's favourite place was sad too, desolate, in the winter the dry leaves were like sad, slow footsteps and slow tears falling. I never went back to that garden again after we had gone away from there.

When Norman came to Sunday dinner my wife tried to make everything as nice as she could. He had aged since Madge's death. His coming was a reproach, for I remembered every time I saw him how he had looked the day she died. And I realised too late how much he had loved her, how unselfishly he was able to love. And, unlike me, was able to put her happiness first or tried to, always before his own. And that it was not his fault that Madge did not love him, only his misfortune.

When we sat together in the small kitchen to have our meal I had to turn away from Norman, I could not look at him. In the long silences between the fragments of conversation, I often found myself thinking of the big house and the household in which I had grown up and become the kind of man I now was.

The plastic table cloth and the dishes of cabbage and cheap mince were quite unlike the things we had been accustomed to having. Norman tried asking us a riddle, he asked Elise, 'What is the difference between an elephant and a pillar box?' His good tempered face bulged at the cheeks with his smile, but Elise could not answer riddles. She laughed and slid under the table. My wife tried to laugh and answer repeating the riddle and trying to hold the table cloth from slipping.

'What's the difference between — oh I give up.'

'I'll never ask you to post my letters then, ' Norman laughed. We all tried to laugh and a silence followed. The little house was full of such silences. Without the regular rhythm of the metronome there seemed to be no heart beating in the house, no singing came from behind closed doors, no striving piano starting bravely and stopping for correction and starting again.

I longed for Madge and I longed for the cello. I wanted the old house and the devotion of its occupants, and my life, as it was, in spite of all the complications.

Norman took his plate with its second helping of pale overcooked vegetables.

'That's good for a growing boy,' he said, smiling. To avoid looking at him, I got up to close the bedroom door.

Elise must have spent the morning pulling things out from the cupboard. Clothes and shoes were scattered and a broken chair lay on its side. Kicked up on the end of the bed, as if with some life of their own, was a pair of knee length leather boots. The long sharp heels, as if obeying some cruel passion, were caught in the white bed-cover.

I sat down again. Norman continued to eat his dinner. I turned towards the window and stared across the desolate view to the tall chimney of the hospital laundry. It seemed to sway very slightly above the swaying ring of trees. The hospital was completely hidden by trees; Norfolk Island pines, kurrajong, jacaranda and flame trees. Secluded somewhere within this green ring were men and women who knew no life other than that within the buildings, the gardens and the park belonging to the hospital. A high wall surrounded the hospital, though from our kitchen window, the wall was not visible. The bedroom door would not stay latched, with a tiresome click it swung open. On the bed the boots kicked. Norman ducked his head to fill his kind mouth with a bent forkful of boiled cabbage. Outside, in the distance, the chimney and the trees swayed. From the harbour down below, in front of the house, came the mournful farewell of a ship putting out to sea.

As on other Sundays I stopped looking at my immediate surroundings and looked back, I turned my thoughts back to the old house. Anyone passing that house could never, at the time when I was living there, have known or understood anything of what was happening there.

II

'There's better ways of killing a bee than drowning it dead in honey,' said my uncle carefully lifting the insect from the jam.

'Yes,' my father agreed, 'but this way seems to work.' He watched the bee struggling, its movements were slow and feeble in the sweet stickiness.

The rest of that hot afternoon has faded from my memory but I understand and know now more of how that bee felt.

There is a time every afternoon when the sun moving towards the west sends long shadows across the enchanted paths of the vineyards. It is a time of tranquillity, of clear warm air and there is, too, a sense of reverence for, in the distance, the orchards and the vineyards crossing great space end in a quiet meeting with the sky.

Remembering the tranquillity I set off with my father to go to the house where I was to board for the next few years while I went to school.

The house was old, standing among other old houses. The sun was already behind the gabled roof and the front of the house was in shadow, screened from the road by Moreton Bay fig trees.

On a side lawn there was a magpie trying to be unconcerned about its young one. The young magpie, complaining, followed the parent bird. For a few minutes it forgot its parent and tried to eat a small piece of paper. It cocked its head, turning to look first in one direction and then in another. It made stupid movements and even more stupid contented noises as it settled itself in a make believe nest. The parent bird moved on to a temporary freedom and found something to eat and at once was followed again by the overgrown fledgling.

'Jacob!' my father called to me.

I turned away from the birds and hurried after him. The shaded garden was filled with the petulance of the big, idiot, baby bird.

I shivered. The house reminded me of an Austrian Schloss I had seen once in a picture book, especially the broken steps and the crumbling arches of the courtyard. As we walked round to the back, all the corners and edges of the house seemed to soften in a sudden last light from the sun. A final caress, perhaps even a blessing.

Through an open window came the sound of a piano, the first phrases of a Beethoven sonata, tender and thoughtful, hesitating and pausing for correction. Someone was practising, faltering, and after a pause, starting again. I waited beside my father. The piano spilled into the quietness.

'It is good,' my father said, 'a lovely touch and tone.' My father wanted me to study music and was placing me with this family for this reason and because the school was near. The headmaster had recommended the house, he had agreed that boarding school life did not suit every boy.

The rat in the room was the property of Waldemar. It was stuck, head and half its body into a loaf of bread. Crumbs

11

were scattered everywhere. Because the room was full of people, I tried to hide my disgust.

'Take Jacob into the garden Louise.' A slender girl, obeying, led the way from the dark sitting-room which was also the rat's.

It was time for the mulberries. At the end of the garden was the tree; it was as big as the house. The leaves were thick and green and the old branches were gnarled and twisted like branches in the pictures in fairy tales. There was a strong scent of fermenting overripe berries. Up in the tree was an enormous boy. He was bigger than anyone else in the house. He was fat and had fair hair. He was Waldemar.

'Which hend you hev?' Waldemar slid down from the branches, his porky face was suddenly close to mine, bursting with squeaky laughter.

'Which hend you hev?' And his two white fists hung before me.

'Which! Which! he squeaked.

'Oh I'm not playing that,' I said.

'Aw, go on! Which hend you hev?' and he waved the white balls of fist up and down. So I tapped the left one and from between the fat, white fingers a cockroach fell kicking into the front of my shirt. Delight burst from Waldemar, he snorted and wheezed and squeaked with laughter; he snapped his fat fingers and choked. With all sorts of noises coming from his clumsy body he scrambled back into the tree only to slide down almost at once. 'Which hend you hev,' he began again and I tried to protest 'Oh no I'm not play—.'

'Open your mouth and shut your eyes,' he insisted. I refused. He pushed a ripe mulberry between my teeth and showered more all about me. Louise was steadily reaching up and picking the berries, so, ignoring Waldemar, I followed her example.

'Jacob!' My father was calling me softly across the garden. 'Jacob.' He had come with Mr Heimbach from the gloomy house to find me. We all stood under the tree with Waldemar rustling and wheezing somewhere above our heads. 'Jacob'

12

my father said, 'I have to go now. Mr Heimbach will be your music teacher. Work hard! I must go.'

'The cello,' Leopold Heimbach said and he bowed slightly as he took both my mulberry stained hands in his own. 'I will make you a Prince of the cello!' He smiled and his smile was edged with gold tipped teeth.

'My sisters, Heloise and Rosa, they will cherish you and teach you, and Louise — Louise you will supervise, *nicht wahr*?' He turned from me still smiling in his complicated way of speaking, and bowed to my father. 'We shall, as you see, all take part in Jacob's education and his voice deepened with significance, 'we shall all take part in his life.' And he led the way, with dignity, across the uneven broken remains of the courtyard and my father followed.

Waldemar teased unmercifully, he put his rat on my chair. Louise pushed it off quickly and it lay stuck in its loaf, the grey pink tail fleshily horrible and apparently lifeless in an indolent curve on the floor boards. Waldemar teased and threatened. He was a big, flabby boy and his hair was thin and wispy, he had a pink, fat face and a selfish little mouth and he dropped his food everywhere.

'Go on punch Waldemar!' Leopold Heimbach said to me as we left the tea table. 'With Waldemar you will strengthen your body,' he smiled kindly upon me. 'And then your education will be complete,' he said.

In the evening I felt homesick thinking of my father on his solitary journey. I thought of him turning off the road at the corner where the sand track went off at right angles and disappeared almost at once into the vines, only to appear like a white tape stretching between the more distant vineyards. From the beginning of the track it was possible to see an enormous fig tree which filled a sandy patch in front of our house. Scales hung in the tree and a trestle table stood in front of it. We sold grapes and melons to people on Sundays. I guessed my father must be nearly at the tree by now.

'Come on,' Louise said, 'I will show you the house.' There

seemed to be innumerable rooms in a kind of dark confusion. She ran her hands over the keys of a piano in one room and continued the scale on a piano in the next room. Music stands and violins in cases were neatly arranged by the wall. The main hall and a big room downstairs had been made into one large hall. The staircase went up from there. The kitchen, thoroughly scrubbed and bare, lay behind this hall In spite of the shabbiness of the house the staircase was still graceful with polished bannisters and the carpet was patterned with roses on a mossy green background. Everywhere it was very clean.

There was a family sitting-room in front on the first floor. We all had rooms from a passage going horizontally across the house. There seemed to be more rooms and furniture of an old fashioned sort than we could all use.

'What's up there?' I asked Louise. The next staircase was of unvarnished wood and seemed to go on up into darkness.

'Oh, we never go up there, the roof leaks dreadfully,' Louise laughed and went to call gently to Waldemar that he should go to bed.

That night, vaulted in brown linoleum, I longed to be back in the narrow room at the side of the weatherboard house where the vines grew right up to the window. Often there were leaves in my room, sometimes crumpled dying and yellow and sometimes fresh leaf-green leafiness in the damp evenings, shaking profiles of little well-bred leaf faces, silhouettes, nodding and shaking with quiet laughing, and sighing tiny fragments of messages which could never be understood in the tremulous movement.

I longed so much to be home again that I got up and dressed and went down the stairs to the front door. The door was locked and I could not open it. I went back up in the big, dark house in despair and then I thought of Waldemar. His room was littered with clothes and stuffed toys. I stumbled to his bed side. Waldemar smelled of milk and biscuits like a small child.

'Waldemar,' I whispered. 'Waldemar unlock the bolt for

me.'

He refused to wake up. I shook his bulky body.

'Waldemar, I'll send you back a piece of curved wood.'

'What'll I do with it?' he asked, his huge shape rising.

'You could hold it in your hand,' I said softly. 'Please unlock —' So at last he agreed and we crept down to the big hall and Waldemar unlocked the door and I started out to find my way back home.

It was very dark and the night was uneasy. I was afraid to set off, but my wish to get home was so strong I could not give it up. I walked along by hedges and fences, timidly in a strange land, to the main road. Here I crossed over and began to walk more boldly. Almost at once a truck pulled up alongside.

'Whatever's a little kid like you doing on the road at this this time of night?' the driver called out. When I explained where I was going to get back home he said he would take me.

'Well, that's not far out of my way, but don't you go making a habit of this!' he said. With relief I sat up beside him.

It was beginning to be light when we reached the road bridge. I could smell the river. Often when we crossed this bridge in winter my father complained that all his topsoil was being washed down from the vineyards. In the summer we went swimming from the mud banks, the grass being worn away by so many feet. My father walked on the water with thin, white bent legs.

Half asleep I climbed down from the truck at the place where the sand track went off from the main road. I set off running as fast as I could.

On both sides the vines looked like ragged little people kneeling on the earth to pray. I thought I'd ask them one day why they prayed. 'I'm glad to see you praying, I'm nearly home.' I wanted to call out 'I'm nearly home,' but I had not breath.

I could see the giant fig tree. I ran without breathing. The dog came running from the shed.

'Don't bark so, Freda,' I could only moan at her.

15

Uncle Otto appeared in a square of light. The door was open behind him.

'Why Jacob! What are you doing here?' He was surprised. His legs were white and crooked like the legs of a goat under his night shirt. I ran up to him, crying, 'I want to come home.' My uncle caught me and held me to him. Freda jumped all round us. She licked my face and hands.

'No and no!' Uncle Otto said. 'You must not go in and disturb him. You must not wake your father. Aunt Mitzi and I have come over to keep him company for a few days. He is very lonely without you, but he wants you to go to school.'

'It was your idea!'

'No and no it was not! Your father wants you to study music; you have the gift, it is from your mother. She never had the chance to study. She used to sing. You can remember your mother singing?'

'No! Well, yes I can.' My tears started to come again.

'Don't go upsetting your father,' Uncle Otto held my arm. 'Now don't cry! Come in the kitchen. Quiet now!'

In the kitchen I sat on a chair while Uncle pulled on his clothes and his boots. It seemed as if I had been away for years. The kitchen looked small, but the smell had not changed. I told him I wanted to stay at home and be as I used to be. I told him about the house and about Waldemar.

'There's a rat too,' I said. He nodded his white head. He cut a thick slice of white bread and poured melon jam from an old tin over it. He held it out to me, the jam dripping, on a folded newspaper.

'Eat,' he said, 'and you will feel better.' I ate a second piece and drank the hot tea Uncle Otto made. My uncle, like my father, always smelled of new cut wood and oil. I wished I could be little forever, playing in the dark shed, near my father and able to rush out into the sunlit vineyard whenever I wanted to.

'A man can't go backwards in his life,' Uncle Otto said.

16

'A man has to go on and learn new things. He has to go out from his home. You have to learn at school. You can't leave before you start!' He spoke gently and seriously. 'I'll drive you back to town. It is better not to miss the first day at school.'

'I want to get something from the shed.'

'You're not tricking me are you?' he wanted to know. 'You're not going to hide somewhere out there? It's dark you know.'

I ran off quickly, knowing my way, between the vines to the yard which was stacked with oil drums and enormous barrels rotting. I went to the shed where my father made the staves. I felt about for one of the curved pieces of wood for Waldemar.

On the way back I must have slept. In no time my uncle was pushing me out of his car. He pointed to the gateway hidden in the trees.

'In you go! Quick! Stay and do your lessons,' he said in his low voice, 'learn your music, practise! And before long, all is finished!' He snapped his fingers. It was his way of showing how quickly the time would go.

The magpies were on the lawn, the mother bird was looking for food and the young one was still wailing. I ran up to the house. The front door was open. Someone had been sweeping. The sound of a piano came from behind one of the closed doors upstairs. I made my way quietly through the big hall to the kitchen at the back. I could smell coffee.

'I got my chicken livers up the Terrace,' Aunt Heloise, whose face was shapeless and crumpled in the morning, was speaking to Tante Rosa softly. She spoke softly, Louise explained to me, because Rosa had a headache sometimes in the mornings. Tante Rosa walked stiffly like a grenadier. She held her head erect and hardly moved it, as if it hurt to move it. Louise explained that probably Tante Rosa would have to lie down soon, it was something to do with her blood pressure. Then Heloise would wear the keys at her waist and unlock the sideboard later to get sugar biscuits and honey for Waldemar.

17

'I got my chicken livers up the Terrace when they were only ten cents a pound,' Heloise waited for Rosa's approval.

'Tante Rosa makes better liver pâté then Heloise,' Louise whispered to me taking off her blue overall and hanging it on a nail behind the door. 'But today Heloise will make it because of Rosa's head.'

There was a dreamlike quality about being one of them in the kitchen at the beginning of my first day. It was still very early in the morning and already a great deal of scrubbing and cleaning had been done. Either they did not know I had been absent in the night or they chose to say nothing about it.

The girls from St Helena's College were already assembling in the Hall. I associated from the very first, their early arrival with the smell of coffee.

'Now that you are here.' Louise whispered to me as we took our places at the edge of the group of school girls, 'we shall have real coffee for our breakfast after singing class.'

'What do you mean?' I was excited about these secret conversations with this beautiful girl. But Louise only nudged me into silence as Leopold Heimbach appeared on the stairs. He came down slowly. He was dressed neatly, his fine white hair brushed carefully back from his forehead.

'We shall continue with the Requiem Mass of Wolfgang Amadeus Mozart.' Leopold smiled upon us, and in a few minutes, the singing lesson had started with Leopold singing alone.

> *'Tuba mirum spargens sonum —*
> *The last loud trumpet's spreading sound*
> *Shall through the place of tombs be blown*
> *to summon all before the throne.'*

He paused, pointed a long finger at me and gave me the note 'throne — Ah sing to la,' he intoned, Louse nudged me and I opened my mouth and heard my own voice, I was still soprano, ring out in the hushed room.

And then we sang together the quartet,

'Tuba mirum spargens sonum —
The last loud trumpet's spreading tone,
Shall through the place of tombs be blown,
To summon all before the throne
Then shall the judge his throne attain,
And every secret sin arraign
Till nothing unavenged remain.'

And then the *Rex tremendae,* a chorus of all the girlish voices swelled into the hall:

'King of tremendous majesty!
who savest, whom thou saves, free.
Thou fount of pity, save Thou me.'

'It is written,' Leopold said, 'that this work reveals the innermost spirit of its author. Sing! Sing and reveal the innermost spirit! Sing!' Tante Rosa played the few notes on the oboe representing the last trumpet and Leopold sang in clear tenor.

'Tuba mirum spargens sonum
And every secret sin arraign
Till nothing unavenged remain.'

Aunt Heloise, her plump little hands and demure mouth reminding of the folding and patting and pinning behind the closed doors where the sewing machine was, played the piano. Her fat, little hands moved with competence over the keys, sometimes pausing to wait for correction of a false note or a false start, or sometimes increasing in speed to keep up with the singers.

It was not so with Tante Rosa, she played with severe precision. I discovered later, she led singers, the family quartet or the solo violinist with slight, jerky movements of her narrow head.

Of course Leopold excused Rosa, by all means, *'natürlich* to lie down with her head. And again he led the singing, everybody singing together, even my solo parts, repeating and repeating striving towards perfection.

19

And afterwards the girls, rustling in their school dresses, left and we had rolls and coffee in the kitchen sitting on the freshly scrubbed chairs. Waldemar wandered in pink and sleepy. I gave him the piece of curved wood when we were alone in the hall.

'What is it?' he asked me.

'The stave I promised you.' I explained. But he did not seem to remember. He was pleased with the wood though and stood there holding it as I set off for my first day at the school.

III

'*Du der ich nicht sage, dass ich bei Nacht*
weinend liege.'

Leopold is setting Rilke to the piano and Louise is standing
beside him singing, stopping and starting at his request,

> *You, whom I do not tell that at night*
> *I lie weeping*
> *Whose being tires me*
> *like a cradle*
> *You who do not tell me when you wake*
> *for my sake.*'

Heloise, behind folded doors, sits sewing. A customer will
be received shortly. Respectfully. The ordered household kept
scrupulously clean, resounds with the two pianos. Tante Rosa,
a pupil in both rooms, stands in the doorway conducting

21

scales and arpeggios nodding her head stiffly, first in one direction and then in the other.

My first days in the house went by quickly in singing and in school work. After a few weeks it seemed as if I had lived there a long time.

Later on I was to learn in a moment of strange intimacy with Aunt Heloise things, whispered from the folds of her nightdress, which I knew nothing about all the time I was living in the house. She told me then, too, that her legs often ached, her veins were swollen, secretly swollen and hidden. Hadn't I noticed how long she wore her skirts? She asked this with a certain coyness suiting the occasion.

As a boy I saw her, every day, help Leopold to arrange his varicosed legs in a position of supreme comfort on the soft pillows of the chaise-longue, and I did not know then, when I saw her doing this, how much she wished her own legs could rest alongside. Her own legs were from necessity, though my coming into the household as a boarder and pupil had removed certain financial worries, under the piano or under the sewing machine, the treadle animating the quivering short, fat legs as they tapered suddenly into her tiny, stupid, fat feet.

The rat in its cage sang softly and busied itself in shreds of crumpled newspaper. Waldemar talked to his rat and showed off some of his own unusual qualities. He could do great long burps and say 'Hullo' in the middle of the terrible harsh rumbling noises. He could bend his thumbs in every direction and could crack his finger joints sharply. He often disturbed music lessons with these accomplishments. Louise seemed to care very much for Waldemar. She was gentle and tender with him, clearing up his messes and running for freshly laundered clothes for him almost as if she replaced his mother. And to her father and aunts she was gentle and tender. She was always obedient, and at the same time, quietly explained their ways to me. I often pictured to myself the kind of beautiful woman her mother must have been. And yet this mother of Louise was also the mother of Waldemar. There was something mysterious and Louise did not explain this.

'Have you a photograph of her?' I asked Louise one afternoon.

'No,' she said.

Rosa and Heloise never spoke about her, neither did Leopold. Her birthdays must have come and gone every year in the household and no flower was ever placed on the lace-covered table in memory of her.

Waldemar's teeth were horribly decayed and, in front, he had two false ones. He overcame his difficulties with toffee, which he loved, by removing the teeth and their crooked wires and placing them carefully, like deformed and grotesque jewelery, on the table cloth in front of him. Sometimes at meal times, these food encrusted teeth made me feel sick, and I could not swallow my food.

Tante Rosa was sharp and said, 'Eat what's set before you!' I thought Tante Rosa disliked me. It was Aunt Heloise, on that strange unforgettable night later on, who told me that Tante Rosa was not angry, only afraid if I did not eat, because my father paid well for me to be there.

It was delightful to me that Louise, in spite of certain responsibilities, was considered one of the children. Often after dinner we were dismissed together.

'Fetch my two red pills,' Leopold said in the evenings and Louise fetched them. Coloxyl with Danthron, even Leopold's laxatives were as if taken from the mythology and set to music. Leopold and his sisters sat in the large sitting-room with their lace covered little tables on which were mirrors and clocks and china ornaments. They sat, separated by tiny rustling draughts, in large armchairs listening to Brahms until it was time to go to bed. Waldemar often slept early. Often his large body, in repose, had to be roused from the back verandah or the hall floor where he had, from his own strange thoughts, drifted on into sleep. Gently Louise woke him and sent him to bed and after that, though I was four years younger, she treated me as an equal. In that magic hour she became a child and we played with dolls, looked at picture books or chased each other about the house and into the darkness of the overgrown garden.

Louise sat on the crumbling wall of the courtyard; she bit an apple. I loved the way her two top front teeth protruded a very little. I watched her eating the apple, her teeth shone in the dusk.

'Leopold says your voice is breaking already,' she said. I had no reply to this. I had heard the disappointment in Leopold's comment in the morning about my voice disappearing, he had been so pleased with the clear boyish voice and so suddenly, after a few weeks, I seemed to be changing.

'It's just your age,' she said kindly. 'When will you be fourteen?'

'At Christmas.' I told her.

'What are you staring at?'

'You.'

'Why?'

'Because —'

'Because?'

'Because I, well just because you —'

'Do you think I'm pretty Jacob?'

'Of course I do, of course you are.'

'You look at me as if you like me rather.'

'But I do!' I cried.

'Would you like to marry me one day?'

I thought she was mocking me.

'Perhaps,' I said, though I wanted to say, 'Yes of course I'll marry you.'

'Only perhaps? Oh Jacob!'

'I do want to marry you, if you'll have me.' I said.

She slipped from the wall and hugged me.

'I made you a ring,' she said, 'out of my own hair. See it is plaited and woven especially for you. I made it. Try

24

it on.'

The ring fitted me and I wore it from that day on; often I rubbed the soft, firm, dark hair with my thumb and was consoled by it.

Every day I went across to the school and every day I was back in my strange new home, which had so quickly taken me in to itself, before the bell for the end of the afternoon had finished ringing at school.

Waldemar was always waiting for me. He teased me, every day he had some fresh trick to play on me.

'Jacob! Tante Rosa wants you,' he spoke in a thick voice, hard to understand.

'Where?'

'She says to wait in her room upstairs.'

So I climbed the staircase and went to Tante Rosa's room and stood in the dark, severe place not daring to look about me, wondering why Tante Rosa wanted me, dreading her coming. Would she question me about something? Give me medicine? A suppository perhaps? I stood shivering for some time and then heard Waldemar dying on the stairs, choking and laughing, squeaking and wheezing and, when I went on the landing Waldemar could hardly speak, his fat body shook with mirth. Tante Rosa wasn't even at home he managed to tell me at last.

As the stranger, the boarder, in this family, I was just right for these tricks of Waldemar's. If the family were distinguished by their musical and academic qualities, then Waldemar had distinctions of a different kind. For him the sun shone in the mornings, the afternoons and the evenings; his days were unclouded and irresponsible. He crammed his little mouth with sugar biscuits and knocked his milk over. He trod on his aunts' feet and defied his father, grimacing stupidly at authority. But all was pardoned with love and humility. Waldemar was cherished with a devotion in which we all took part, for Waldemar was an idiot.

He slobbered and he smelled and wherever he was not wanted, there he was. He tormented me with dead mice and worms and I quickly lost patience, especially as I had a great deal of homework to do and wanted to finish it quickly to be free for my play time with Louise.

'Go on Jacob,' Leopold said, 'slap the naughty Waldemar! Punch the Naughty Boy! Slap him hard!' Tante Rosa and Aunt Heloise nodded and smiled at me over their crochet. It was that hot, still hour after Sunday lunch and we were all in the big sitting-room upstairs.

'Put the covers on the mirrors Louise,' Tante Rosa said. 'The glare is bad today.' Louise did as she was told, gently drawing the old-fashioned plush cases over the gilt-edge oval mirrors, she drew the curtains a little so that the room seemed cooler suddenly. I turned the page of my book and Waldemar, who was mimicking me, made a grotesque movement copying my own. I tried to look at Louise but she had taken up her handwork and did not look at me. Sometimes I felt she was ashamed of this younger brother. He was my age though physically very much larger. At the time I did not realise how devotion can be learned, taught by example, but it became clear to me later that this was how it was in this family.

Waldemar hid behind doors and jumped on me. He mocked my accent, the exaggerated Australian accent of the central European who is trying to fit in. Waldemar himself, with his big tongue and wet mouth, spoke very indistinctly, with a limited vocabulary and had himself a foreign accent. He spoke the stilted English of his father and his aunts. He saw so few people in his sheltered life that he was more of a foreigner than I was. Because of his imperfections, when he mocked me, he annoyed me and his messiness and clumsy obstinacy and his perpetual presence made me furious. I had never felt such anger before and I was afraid of it. I was homesick too and his mocking and teasing only made this homesickness more acute.

There were times when I longed to be back with my father in the vineyard, especially this hot Sunday afternoon; I kept thinking back and trying to recapture moments which had really ceased to exist before I had left there. In my dreams of the vineyard I pictured myself going out among the vines to the place where my mother always stood in the tranquillity of the afternoon, shading her eyes with her hand and looking over the long lines of vines across to the low hills. When I stepped into this dream I allowed myself to forget she had been dead for some years.

My parents were elderly when I was born. My father had come with my mother and my mother's family some twenty years earlier and I grew up among these people who were foreigners and learned English from them. It was a strange language for them so my accent was strange. And this is what Waldemar mocked when he mocked me.

On Sundays my father worked all day in the gloomy, corrugated iron shed. Barrels and casks cascaded, metal bands rang and the curved wood yawned and yielded as I watched him and, when I was tired of that, I played on the paths between the gnarled vines and their tender growth.

'What hev you to read?' Waldemar kept asking me questions. 'What hev you?'

'Go on Jacob!' Leopold urged me pleasantly. 'Build your muscle, give him a punch. Punch Waldemar!'

Leopold left his chair and pranced gracefully across the floor in the attitude of a boxer with his arms raised. Fondly he tapped my shoulder.

'Bravo! Bravo!' Aunt Heloise clapped her little, fat hands. Waldemar danced and ducked before my chair. He kept putting out a hand, tapping my head and then my nose and then he pulled my book away. I flew out of my armchair, the room shook and I punched Waldemar. My fist, in a knot, sank into his fat chest. He gave a gasp and his pink, porky face changed colour. It became a dull, soft red and his little eyes filled with tears which squirted out as if his eyes were bursting. And with a soft moan he fell forward. Everyone clapped.

'Bravo! Bravissimo!'

And then Louise cried out, running forward to her brother

27

as their mother might have run.

'He's really hurt!'

'He can't be!'

'Where are you hurt Waldi? Where do you hurt my Darling?'

Leopold and Tante Rosa hurried across the room, and more slowly, Aunt Heloise followed them. And all the time Louise had not raised her eyes to look at me. They were all bent over him, trying to raise him, fondling him, caressing him, with their hands and with their voices trying to restore to him what I had taken from him.

I was suddenly all alone on the outskirts of this frantic little group. The room seemed darker and more lonely and I went away to hide alone in my bedroom leaving them to discover by themselves that I had killed Waldemar.

The pods were snapping on the creeper outside the window of my room.

Pod Snap

Snap Pod

Pod Pod Snap Snap

Snap Snap Pod Snap Pod Snap Pod.

Louise came along to find me. I was not hidden at all, I was sitting quite still on the edge of my bed.

'How hot your room is!' she complained. 'You have forgotten to pull down the blind!' I sat still, fear had made me stiff. I could not move my face.

'Father sent me to tell you to come down,' she said. I kept looking at the floor, I thought she would be looking down too to avoid me. She bent down and looked into my face.

'Come down Jacob!'

The pods in the afternoon heat were still snapping.

'What's that noise?' Louise turned as if disturbed.

'The pods on the creeper.' My voice would hardly come out.

'Do they always make that noise?' she asked. 'Only when it's hot I suppose,' she answered her own question. 'It's seed

dispersal, remember?'
She pulled me off the bed.
   'Come downstairs Jacob.'
   'I can't.'
   'Of course you can.'

The table at the end of the hall was laid for dinner, the
white cloth with the polished glasses and silver gave an
immediate sense of reassurance.
   An old man was sitting by the narrow window.
   'He is the doctor,' Louise whispered.
   'Some tea Louise, for Jacob, before dinner,' Leopold stood
up, 'plenty of sugar,' he called, 'and some jam. You would
like jam wouldn't you Jacob?' He caressed my shoulder with
his exceptional hands and he stood me in front of the old
man. He kept his hands on by shoulders.
   'Waldemar died from heart failure,' the old doctor leaned
forward, 'let me explain, his heart was too small for his big
body. Do you understand? His brain also was too small.
Your punch, the doctor gave me a playful poke, 'your punch
coincided with the failure of his heart. That is all,' the old
man sat back disappearing into the narrow alcove.
   Louise came with a laden tray. Everyone was in the hall,
their chairs back near the walls. Everyone agreed with the
doctor, they nodded their heads murmuring their agreement.
Waldemar had not long to live they told each other softly,
his heart was too small, he had outgrown his heart, it could
have failed him at any time. The gentle voices came in waves
from the sides of the room, softer and then louder, like music.
As if we were all in a long, drawn-out dream together, agreeing
over and over again. And in the same dream the old doctor
nodded forwards falling asleep.
   They were so quiet and kind. The pod snapping was over.
I kept looking round for Waldemar or for some of his broken
toys but there was nothing of his lying about.
   'Eat your jam,' Louise crouched beside my chair. 'Do you
like it? Tante Rosa made it.' There was something white,

ground and mixed into the dark red jam. I messed it about with the spoon.

'What is it?'

'Eat,' she said, 'it is a sedative for you, you must have it.' She pressed my arm. 'It is a sed-a-tive, it will help you.'

Tante Rosa sat in my room. There was a wonderful quietness. Outside there was coolness and the timid rustling of the creeper.

In the night I heard someone crying. I thought it was Waldemar crying in the pain I had given him. I could not bear the crying. I tried to call out. I seemed to be standing beside my own bed watching myself. Tall and taller, I was like a tower looking down on my tiny bed. The crying became a howling. The crying came from the bearskin rug, so close, and then from far off as if across a wide river. And all the time I looked down giddily from an immense height.

'It is only the sedative.'

Tall, narrow Tante Rosa stood in the doorway. Behind her were lights moving and footsteps. Someone coming down the second staircase where no one ever went. Why should they come down from there? Aunt Heloise was behind Rosa.

'He sleeps still,' Tante Rosa said.

'Thanking God he was not disturbed,' Heloise said in a low voice. 'No one will know what happened. Rosa!' she said, 'it will be more for us to do.'

'Never mind! We can manage,' Rosa said in a sharp whisper. 'We can manage. And if we cannot then he will have to go. That is all. Quite simple. And now, not another word!'

The morning brought no clear recollection of the night. My head was heavy, the purple creeper made my head ache. I choked and could not sing. Leopold nodded.

'You may leave the class Jacob,' he said.

Louise said, 'Would you like me to walk to the school with you?' I cried like a little boy and I was ashamed.

After this I did not go to school any more but had all my lessons in the house, supervised by Tante Rosa. When she had to disappear because of her headaches or because of the mysterious things she did, Louise sat beside me patiently explaining the tilt of the world and listening to my muttered recitation of tables and French verbs. And more and more time was devoted to my music.

IV

I grew very quickly. I had been nearly a year with them. It was as if I had been there all my life. Suddenly I was taller than Louise but always four years younger, nothing could change that. My father was pleased with my progress. He did not come but Leopold wrote him reports in the form of letters. I was asked to write, I hesitated so Louise told me what to write. 'Dear Father, I am well. I hope you are too, your loving son Jacob.'

In the mornings, the girls from St Helena's assembled. The Requiem was progressing. Leopold led the girlish voices in and out of the experience,

> *'Lacrymosa dies illa —*
> *Oh day of weeping, day of woe ...'*

We were now singing the solo part and the chorus.

The household took part in the singing; sometimes Tante Rosa allowed herself to leave early because of other duties. Afterwards, when the girls had gone, there was the coffee. The sharp, warm smell of the coffee together with the singing excited me. Louise and I raced to the kitchen and, while Tante Rosa was busy elsewhere, Aunt Heloise never minded if we dropped pieces of fresh bread into our coffee cups and sucked the succulent lumps from our spoons.

Before lessons started there was a tremendous sweeping and cleaning of the shabby house. Louise did most of this, she wore a blue apron pulled tightly round her. I thought she looked lovely in the apron, slender and strong at the same time. While pretending not to, I often watched her as she bent over the tables, scrubbing and scraping or, as she leaned into the sink, scouring pans and washing cups and dishes. Aunt Heloise went out early and came back flushed and breathless and, as soon as she appeared, Louise put aside her broom and came rushing to the shopping bags and pulled out packages eagerly, 'Chicken livers, Polish cucumbers, sesame bread! We never had such good things since ages!' she squeezed my arm and her eyes sparkled.

Pupils came to the house and the continual Beethoven Sonata with Leopold counting softly beside the piano was a gentle background to my problems in algebra and geometry.

At the time of Waldemar's death the jacarandas were in flower, tumultuous clouds of violet blue, a profusion of flowerlets falling all the time so that it was as if the trees were in flower from the earth to the sky. Louise danced on the fallen flowers. She picked them up and put them on her fingers and thumbs and wagged her hands at me. Later on the mulberries began to come. I avoided the big tree. I did not mourn Waldemar, it was more a kind of uneasiness as if I might find him in the tree.

No one spoke of Waldemar. His clothes and toys had all disappeared from the rooms. I couldn't help expecting him to be waiting behind a door for me and I wondered if the others felt this too.

Nothing was said; and no one said, 'Today was Waldemar's birthday,' and no one said, 'on this day last year Jacob punched Waldemar and killed him.'

There was never a hint of reproach shown to me and never any sadness.

I met Tante Rosa on the landing. She was coming, the Grenadier, from the plain, upper staircase. It was dark on the landing, just one square of light on the polished boards, there was a small window there facing out to the west at the foot of the steep unvarnished stairs. Tante Rosa, erect and stern, stepped down into the golden square, she was carrying a pail.

'Let me carry it down please,' I offered at once. The rosebud lid rattled as her hand clutched.

'Never mind!' she said sharply. 'It is not heavy, thank you.' As she walked stiffly by I thought the smell of the pail was familiar. I asked Louise in the evening.

'Oh those dirty old pails!' she said, 'they need cleaning properly, just for roof leaks now. Silly old pails!' She drew me out to the dusk on the back verandah, the trees in a ring were restless and black on an inflamed sky.

'Here,' Louise whispered, 'something I have made you. Another ring! See it is again with my own hair. Change the ring on your finger. See if the new one fits.' Her whispering was a delight it had a dream-like quality and the evening was wonderful with Louise's soft laughter.

In the kitchen Aunt Heloise had the key, as Rosa was busy, and she unlocked the cupboard and filled my hands with sugar biscuits.

'Have one,' I offered my hands to Louise but she shook her head. I was able to eat them all quite easily and I licked up the crumbs, Aunt Heloise nodded at me and smiled.

The evenings were different now as Louise always had pupils and I practised the cello.

My cello kept crying into my heart. When I played the cello Leopold listened and counted softly. Sometimes he changed into a dressing-gown and played the piano and I played the first cello from Schubert's Quintet in C. Sometimes we all played, Tante Rosa and Aunt Heloise — violins, Louise the viola, myself first cello and Leopold second cello. It was not often we were all together for long enough. Rosa and Heloise had their work which took them to different parts of the house. The treadle of the sewing machine rumbled incessantly, muffled behind the folded doors. Louise had her pupils and I had to study.

When I played the cello and the cello hesitated, poised on a single note so pure and restrained and lovely, I closed my eyes with an exquisite love of the cello. I was in love with the cello.

Leopold stopped me.

'You are virtuoso,' he said to me in a low tone and went back to the piano. He was very thoughtful.

'Continue,' he said and he played the piano, once more counting softly while I played.

Waldemar loved to eat little pickled cucumbers, he dipped them into the honey. He had his own honey jars and he liked to push his fingers into clear golden sweetness, he loved honey. I remembered I had not seen his honey jars since he was dead. Everything else of his had gone and the rat too. There was not even a footmark or a dirty hand mark left from Waldemar.

I tried to take the broom from Louise, she was sweeping the rough boards on the verandah. Often I felt I ought to help her, so I took the broom.

'But no!' she cried and held the broom close to her blue apron. 'Sweeping is not for you!' She refused to let me help though she was rushing through the sweeping and washing and cleaning. Already the first pupils had come and, from beyond the softness of the Beethoven, came the clear sounds of a voice practising to 'la' up the scale and down and up one half tone higher.

Two boys came across from the school and we exchanged a few embarrassed phrases standing together in the scrubbed kitchen. Aunt Heloise nodded and smiled at the boys and gave them apples to put in their pockets. Tante Rosa came in.

'Time for your study Jacob.'

The boys said they would come back later after school.

'Jacob will be practising the cello then and must not be disturbed,' Tante Rosa told them and led them with her Grenadier march to the front door. The boys never came again to see me and their visit was, in a sense, my last contact with the outside world. From then on I never went anywhere.

I thought of myself simply as a student of music and I looked upon myself as a murderer and considered my imprisonment quite in order. I had no wish to be free. I preferred not to go to school, and, though the house and garden were open to the street, I never went out into the street. I read and studied and lived in the household which seemed to contain all in the way of books and musical instruments and teachers I could ever need.

On my sixteenth birthday Tante Rosa gave me a jar of balm to rub into my hands. She showed me how to scoop up the grease and how to massage my hands and wrists, smoothing the skin and caring for each finger in turn. It gave me pleasure to look at my hands and to care for them in this way. They became more delicate than any hands I had ever seen except for Leopold's, but mine were even smoother and more finely shaped than his. He admired my hands. Sometimes I knew he was looking at them. I found a strange pleasure in making my hands perform for him. While I played, my hands would attract attention by themselves, my wrists turned and the backs of my hands exposed themselves as if to invite comment from Leopold. Sometimes my hands invited Leopold's hands and at these times I noticed his trembled but did not accept the invitation. Often our hands nearly touched, mine moving closer, pirouetting even, and his always restrained. It seemed to me later on that I enjoyed the role of tempter then, however much I came to despise it afterwards.

My hair had not been cut since I came to the house. It

had grown long and soft and fell in slow curls well below my shoulders. Tante Rosa picked up some curls and let them fall.

'You must have haircut,' she said that morning. For the first time for a year I went out with Leopold. I walked beside him along the strange streets. How different the air was suddenly. Nervously I sat in the shabby waiting-room at the barber's shop, I felt everyone was looking at us. Leopold was so elegant and he moved gracefully, he bowed even as we passed people we did not know. To him it was natural, he was not being affected in his manner, not at all. Later on I tried to explain this to Madge, but that was much later on.

We were very quiet together. I wanted to stare at the people in the street.

'It's quite in order to look at people,' Leopold said quietly, 'but one must not turn round and look at them after they have gone by.'

The sensations of having my hair cut were remarkable and I gave myself up to the new experience and to the experience afterwards of running my fingers over the crisp short hair.

'Oh, Jacob's curls!' Louise wailed often and Leopold agreed that my hair should be allowed to grow again,

'To the shoulders,' he said, 'is suitable for the Prince of the cello,' and his smile was like a blessing.

Every week Leopold went to the hospital to conduct a singing class. One day he said I could go with him. There was a path, a short cut, to the place which Leopold explained was a mental institution. The short cut lay across a waste land fringed on one side with dead trees standing, unable to fall, in the still water of a swamp. The place was to me an indescribable horror. It was excavated and pitted, parts of it were filled with cut down trees and the diseased rubble from demolished buildings and there was the terrible stench of household rubbish, dead cats and dead dogs unwanted things deposited here and all pushed to and fro and alternatively covered and uncovered by a whining tractor. I could not believe that the shining brown thing on the machine was a man.

'He is sunburnt,' Leopold explained.

'But his eyes?'

'They are covered with goggles to keep out the glare and the dust.' Leopold made little goggles round his own eyes, with his hands, to show me what he meant. Paper and blown rags hung like horrible curtains on the wire fences and people, bent in half, scurried about in the rubbish.

'They are looking for something good and useful,' Leopold explained.

'Here?'

'Well why not, in everything and in every place there is something useful,' he shrugged shoulders and gave his little unaffected bow towards the pits and the heaps.

Saved things glittered, a long mirror, some glasses, a white bowl, bedsteads were put up and mattresses, the flock coming out, lay rolled on these iron beds, there were books on a makeshift shelf and even clothes hung like ghosts in the smell which made me nearly sick.

'The mirror is cracked.'

'Well of course,' Leopold smiled.

The hospital grounds seemed green and secluded, even peaceful as we walked under an avenue of trees to the buildings. Leopold pointed out the laundry chimney, the patients washed their own clothes he said.

Mostly the patients sang, they had no instruments.

To get to the women we had to go through a long hall with ceilings so high I had to look up into the vaults to be sure they were there. I thought it must be children in this hall because they were all in cots with bars. In the dingy light they seemed to be half asleep. Some sat up, asleep, some stood drowsily hanging over the ends of their cots, some rocked to and fro even banging their heads with rhythmic regularity on the cot bars. They were dressed in white waistcoats buttoned over their nightgowns, tied at the backs with tapes and with long, thick tapes passed under the cots.

'Why is the boy all tied up in ribbon?'

'So he will not fall out,' Leopold replied softly. He strode after the orderly who had the key for the doors at both ends of the long room. I stared at the cots and at the children. I smiled at one boy but he seemed not to notice. Another child pulled at my jacket and I drew away in fear from his expressionless face. They were all so quiet, no one was talking or laughing or even crying.

Only the orderly made a noise; he whistled. Our shoes made a clap, clap on the polished floor and then in shimmering curves, uncontrollable, a voice rang out.

'Why are the children so sleepy?' It was my voice. The orderly said, 'Oh it's their pills makes them sleepy, that's all it is.'

'Pills?' I said, 'why what is wrong with them?' The orderly was bent unlocking the farther door.

'There's nothing wrong with them,' he said, 'they're just idiot children.'

We came to the women then. Mostly they were shapeless, dressed in brown overalls with brown headscarves. They undulated, sitting one alongside another on long benches. Leopold played the piano in there with them and they sang hymns and carols and songs I had never heard before. I could not understand the words. The women seemed pleased to see Leopold. They gathered about him when it was the end of the singing time as if they would try to keep him there. I did not sing and Leopold did not make me. I stared about me and listened to the mournful sounds of their voices. I wondered why Leopold went there, I felt he seemed glad when it was time to leave.

We walked back together across the waste land where the rubbish was and the ghost trees stood holding up their thin arms along the edge of the swamp. I was glad to get away from the desolate place to the sunlit pavements where jacaranda trees again stood in blue pools of fallen flowers.

The sun warmed our backs and, as I walked, I stared at the houses and at the people. There were sprinklers on the lawns and I wanted to take off my shoes and walk on the cool, wet grass.

'Go on then,' it seemed Leopold would allow me to do anything I wanted. He waited with patience while I untied the shoes and pulled off my hot socks. It seemed suddenly as if I could drink through the soles of my feet. I walked on the springing, wet grass, the coolness coming up between my toes and spilling over the tops of my feet.

'I'm glad I'm not in that place,' I said to Leopold and he agreed.

'I'm glad you're not,' he said.

In the evening Louise was preparing for her pupil.

'You know,' I said to her, 'you know something?'

'What?' she said, her long fingers paused between the creamy pages of the Chopin piano studies.

'I think your father is glad I killed Waldemar, so he needn't be in that hospital room,' I said.

'Oh Father has been going there for years,' Louise said lightly. 'It has simply nothing to do with you,' she said 'or with anyone else.' Her pupil was at the front door and Louise left me. She had not really replied to what I had said. And I never tried to say it to her again.

And so I played the cello, pleading and sighing, melodious, elegiac and lovely. The human voice I thought to myself, even in the most moving songs of Schubert or Brahms or Mahler, could not express such exquisite tenderness. I felt a deep love for the cello and I loved Louise. I loved Louise deeply, my love for her was interwoven with the pure sustained love I had for the cello.

Of course she no longer came up with me when I went to bed. We parted every night in front of the armchairs where Tante Rosa and Aunt Heloise were sitting or, if they were busy elsewhere, we stood a moment beside the long wicker chair where Leopold rested his swollen legs in the evenings.

'Goodnight my children,' he gave his blessing.

In the house some bedrooms opened out from each other. Louise had such a room. It was beyond Aunt Heloise's room which, in turn, was guarded by Tante Rosa whose dark, severe room opened off the landing. I had never been in Louise's room. Mostly we had played with her dolls down on the back verandah. My small room had warm sunshine from a west window and, at first, Louise came there often. As we grew older she no longer came except with Tante Rosa on a cleaning expedition or sometimes to hunt for cockroaches with white powder and long steel knitting needles which were poked between the floorboards and behind the moulding of the skirting boards. They chose times to do this when I was with Leopold.

It was Sunday, we were sitting, as usual, together in the large room on the first floor.

'Is this gold thread not just a little vulgar?' Heloise asked Tante Rosa. She spread out the material on her plump knee.

'Hand embroidery can never be vulgar, Rosa replied. She took the tea Louise handed to her. 'Least of all the herring-bone stitch.'

Tante Rosa, with Leopold at the piano, had been singing for us.

'*Deutsche Volkslieder von Johannes Brahms,*' Leopold made the announcement. Rosa sang with unexpected charm, her eyes lighting up and changing so that her whole face had a new expression. As she sang she raised her eyebrows and made little movements with her head suggesting impertinence. Her voice, too, surprised me with its new quality of playfulness quite unlike Tante Rosa as she usually was. It seemed to me that she even looked happy while she sang the folk songs.

Then it was my turn to sing while Rosa played. Leopold, pointing first at me and then at Louise conducted the singing class. We had to sing the song over and over again. Louise, when she sang, had a delightful way of pausing between words; especially it gave me pleasure when she paused, turning her eyes towards me, before the words 'my angel'.

> *'You'll leave me for other girls,*
> *I can certainly imagine that, my angel'*

I loved my lines in the song and I tried to make my voice pure and sweet and tender for her.

> *'Come to me, I'm coming to you,*
> *You must answer me, my angel.'*

Leopold walked to and fro. 'Superb,' he said. 'Once more, start again.'

> *'Good evening. Good evening my sweetheart in*
> *a thousand . . .'*

And then my uncle walked into the room.

'I've been knocking, knocking, knocking down there,' he explained, knocking his bent knuckle into the palm of his other hand. 'No one hears me so I walk in.'

To see Uncle Otto was a surprise. He held up his hands to stop the exclamations of surprise and welcome. He had come he said, talking carefully and emphatically, to bring the news that my father was dead. There had been an accident.

'He was killed instantly,' he said, the news all over in a moment.

'He was killed instantly,' Tante Rosa and Aunt Heloise repeated the words. From the corners of the room came these nodding heads and kind smiles. Tiny soft waves of words repeating and comforting, 'Better dead than half alive.'

'He was killed instantly, you understand,' my uncle said to me while Leopold caressed my shoulders.

I hardly seemed to remember my father. I hardly understood the conversation about the selling of the vineyards.

'The land is very valuable between the main road and the river,' Uncle said. 'You will be a very rich young man. They will be building all over the vineyard.'

'Ah a housing estate!' Leopold understood at once. 'You must thank your uncle, Jacob, for looking after all your affairs.' He continued to stroke my shoulders.

'Thank you,' I began to say. I thought I was going to be sick.

'Quick Rosa! Heloise! The boy is ill,' I heard Leopold's voice somewhere far away. I felt them help me into the chair. Cool, damp cloths were on my face.

'Louise bring something to revive Jacob,' Leopold's voice was very close to me. He was bending over me looking anxious. The tea Louise offered me tasted like an infusion of strange berries. My uncle was sitting opposite.

'You're very kind,' I tried to thank him again.

'Quiet now! You've had a shock. What I have done is nothing. But Mitzi, your Aunt Mitzi is in love with the land,' he sighed. 'Land speculation to tell the truth, it's her life. I think she will burst herself over this sale.'

I thought of Aunt Mitzi as my land agent. What a good cook she was too. I felt tremendous relief. None of it had much to do with me. I was a singer and a cello player, surely that was enough. My face twitched painfully and I had to pretend to laugh. My voice came out much louder than I expected it to.

'I'd like to go out there,' I said.

'Sure. Sure thing,' my uncle said, springing up. 'Can I take him now?'

'Of course. But *natürlich,* he is a man, he can decide what he likes to do.' Leopold put my cello, which I had been playing earlier, gently in its case as if he were putting an overgrown baby to bed.

'Are you well enough to go out?' Aunt Heloise whispered in my ear, 'because if you are not, you can go another time.'

'Come back safely!' Louise laughed. They all laughed saying, 'Come back safely. Come safely back. *Auf Wiedersehen.'*

I kept thinking of Louise. My uncle drove fast. He had a big new car. The streets were all quite strange. I had become accustomed to going only to the hospital with Leopold and to the concert hall where I now played. For that journey we took a taxi.

To make a shield against the crowded streets I tried to think of Louise. She would be washing up the tea cups, possibly she would have put on the blue apron. Everything seemed to be rushing at me, big pictures and advertisements with curious spelling. An eye came towards me and then a bottle and then hands in pairs and singly blue and yellow black on white zigzag circle faces and legs yellow yellow yellow.

'Stop!' I cried aloud to my uncle. 'Take me back home. I won't go there today after all.'

My uncle stopped the car. He stared at me. He looked so frightened that I became more frightened and I screamed. He said afterwards that I screamed, 'I don't remember ever hearing anything like it,' he said when we returned home, 'his face was so white. I thought the air would do him good, but no! and the scream!'

'He will be better soon,' Leopold consoled in the hall.

'I had no idea!' my uncle said.

'It is all right,' Leopold comforted my uncle, 'Rosa and Heloise will see that he rests,' I heard the murmur of their voices. My little bedroom, with the curtains drawn, had never seemed so peaceful and comfortable.

In the evening Louise and I celebrated our engagement. They were all ready for me, waiting in the big calm room, Leopold, Tante Rosa, Aunt Heloise. Louise had on a brown dress, the one I liked best, it was of very fine wool and had a collar of cream lace made by Aunt Heloise.

'Here is my daughter,' Leopold said, he moved Louise towards me, 'for dowry she has two loving aunts and a stupid father!'

Louise and I poured sweet white wine into little glasses and handed them to Tante Rosa and Aunt Heloise and to Leopold and nothing was said about my journey and its abrupt ending.

'Tante Rosa and Aunt Heloise have on their best blouses,' Louise whispered. 'If you can, say something nice about them.' Obediently I bowed to them both and thought of things to say about the blouses.

V

A few days later I went to see the vineyards. I went alone in a taxi. On the way I asked the driver to stop.

I stood on the road bridge and looked at the gentle curve of the river. The brown water was still, it looked deep and cool. I thought of the times, as if in another world, I had gone swimming there with my father and Uncle Otto. On white bent legs, arms flailing, they entered the water and their wet heads came up shining and small.

The quiet trees and dry feathered grasses hung motionless at the edge of the water. Long, brittle flies dipped across to and fro just above the surface. The noise of an aeroplane disturbed the quietness.

'An aeroplane makes a lonely place more lonely,' I told the driver.

'Too right it does!' He was a little man and friendly.

Across on the other side some concrete had been set sharply

at right angles, slab upon slab, jutting awkwardly, unfinished.

'The new bridge,' my driver approved.

Trees had been pushed over and the earth folded back by some immense power. Overhead wires hummed from one wooden pole to the next. Cars and trucks rumbled over our bridge.

'You sick?' my driver seemed anxious. 'You're dead white!'

I could not keep my face still, it moved constantly, first one muscle twitched and then another. It was painful. I turned aside. My dark suit was out of place by the white wooden rails of the bridge. A line of heavy trucks crossed the trembling structure, one after another, the noise became unbearable.

'Change clothes with me,' even with my voice raised, I could not make him hear me. I laughed and, in the silence following the last truck, my laughter hung bellowing growing fainter across the water. Of course he could not give me his clothes in exchange for mine, the quality was different and then there were the sizes. How horrified he would be, I thought.

The road went by the brick works. The kilns were careless shambling ovens as big as houses, built of bricks without mortar. They glowed with new bricks and the stacks of freshly cut firewood glowed with the same apricot colour.

'Turn off here,' I told him. The narrow straight road disappeared in the vineyards. Here and there were small weatherboard houses with iron roofs. Most of them needed painting. I tried to remember names as I saw them chalked on faded boards. I could not recall one face to fit any name.

'Drive slowly here please,' I asked him. I looked at the vines. Some were as if kneeling and praying there on the earth and others were raised, their arms lifted and hoisted over high posts. I thought again of them as I did when I was a child, I imagined them to be slaves with their shoulders lifted too high and lashed to posts. Pale, childish grape bunches hung in secret under the trellised woodwork of the vines.

'Here,' I said, 'turn right.' The stone pillars of the gateway

46

were still there, the wrought iron gates, with our name on, had been removed.

I had not expected to see my father's vineyard burned. The whole way down to the river it was burned. Blackened spines of vines spread out on either side. Wooden pegs marked the sites for shops and houses. The sheds were no longer there; even the barrel, which had been rotting for years because it was too big to move, was gone.

There was an extraordinary beauty in the burned house. Sunlight came through the blackened rafters and patches of light and shade made secret dwellings for memories in rooms which no longer resembled any I had known.

'How quickly everything is destroyed,' I said.

'Too right!' the driver nodded. He respected my bewildered grief.

The scales still hung in the fig tree and the patched table round the base was sturdy. I went down to the river, the little landing stage, without reason for being there, seemed smaller. In the silence I half expected my father's bent, dark figure to emerge.

I walked slowly back to where the driver waited.

'Progress,' he said.

'Yes,' I looked at him. He could have no idea that my mind was more occupied with wealth than with grief. I wanted to talk to him about money and I wanted to talk to him about Louise.

'How about I drive you across to the other road and take you home that way,' he said, 'makes a change. Looks to me as if you need a change.'

He stopped on the hill by an outcrop of granite. We stood between the trees and looked down to the wide plain. Beyond the vineyards was the city and, beyond again, something shone in a deep blue, a joining of the sky and the sea. I had forgotten about the sea. How could I have forgotten!

'You are virtuoso!' Leopold said the words often. Lately he had spoken sadly, saying the time had come for him to give me to the world. Describing circles with his hands. 'You

47

must travel,' he said. 'I would come with you, but alas!' His swollen varicose legs demanded respect. In his heart, he told me, he would accompany me for ever.

Standing beside the taxi driver high up in the fragrance of leaves and earth, I was afraid. Suddenly I was sick.

'That's better!' he said, 'better out than in.'

All night there were storms. Thunder rolled in the distance, coming nearer and retreating. It rained, the first rain, the smell of the earth was sharp like an anaesthetic. The nervous twitch, which twisted my face painfully at times, seemed to take over my whole body. All night I seemed to sleep yet be awake as if leaping and falling; almost asleep and then awake on my comfortable pillows.

After the storm it was no better. The east wind, moaning, went through the house restlessly. The walls and the gables creaked and invisible feet pressed the boards of the stairs. Overhead there was no harmony. I thought I could hear someone crying, someone soothing, something falling and I thought I heard someone coming.

I was afraid of my own face in the mirror. At first it was unrecognizable, shining with sweat and with an expression in my eyes quite unlike what I believed myself to be.

Roses, drenched and sweetly scented, pressed in at my window. Breathing in their sweetness I wished I had only them to think of. Roses and Louise.

I did not know then what I was to discover quite soon.

The tiny chimes of my clock were charming but a painful reminder that hours were passing and I was sleepless. I began to prowl, first to and fro in the small space of my room, and then out on to the landing. I went up the unvarnished staircase and, noiselessly, along the passage. It was not unknown. I had looked before only to find the rooms locked.

The door at the end was not locked. A key was in the keyhole. The door was not latched, a crack of light came from the room. In the passage there was a smell, a sweetness as from a hospital room, a smell of cheap soap and wrapped up fruit mingled with the smells of the body. The warmth of the smell enveloped me as I pushed open the door. I peered in. A chair lay broken in a corner. Some crockery of a coarse kind, I had never seen any like it in the house, lay smashed. In a pool of milk were broken toys and torn up rags and papers. There was no furniture except a plain table and a bed. The disorder was obviously the remains of violence. It must have been a subdued violence, hushed for privacy. On the bed lay an enormous man. His thin, fair hair lay pressed damp on his white forehead. He seemed to be asleep, breathing noisily. His tongue, swollen, protruded from his mouth. His mouth seemed too small to hold the tongue. He was dressed in washed out rags which were tight and torn on his fat body. I looked at him. I could see at once that he was Waldemar.

So Waldemar was alive and lived in this terrible room. Beside the door was the pail with the rosebud lid. And, kneeling beside the bed, holding his head in both hands as if it hurt him, was Leopold.

VI

All at once, the next morning, it was autumn. It was raining and leaves fell from the flame trees. I sat on the verandah. Every now and then I could hear a rustling like footsteps, but no one was coming. It was only the sound of leaves detaching themselves and falling one after another onto the wet earth.

I supposed I must have been dreaming in the night. If I had not been dreaming then I was free. Yesterday, from the hills, I had looked across the land which had brought me a fortune. I had seen beyond it to the sea. Everything yesterday was calm in the sunshine. Calm and clean.

If Waldemar was alive, everything would be different. I wondered what kind of life he had up there in that small room, with the flat windows, under the eaves. I wondered if I would see him again. I felt excited and anxious.

Louise came out to sweep. It was the time of the cleaning.

I sat watching the leaves and listening to the rhythm of the sweeping and to the argument of the doves as they mocked the morning.

'Are you ill?' Louise asked me, her voice as gentle as the doves.

Since our engagement the other evening I had not seen her alone and, because of my new freedom, I wanted to kiss her and hold her close to me. Something much more than the formal embrace and the kiss of betrothal in the presence of Tante Rosa, Aunt Heloise and Leopold.

'Are you ill Jacob?' Louise repeated her question. I got up slowly and I put my arms round her slight body. How the blue apron suited her! In a rush of tenderness I knocked the broom out of her hand. It fell with a noise which brought Tante Rose out on to the verandah.

'Time for your lesson!' she said to me. Louise bent to pick up her broom and I was unable to see her eyes. I could hear Leopold playing a few notes on the piano and I went indoors at once.

When I played the cello I was soothed. I closed my eyes, dwelling on the long sustained note as if I were kissing Louise. Leopold stopped me and took my hand, as if to steady my trembling.

'You are virtuoso,' he said in a low voice. His hand caressed mine. 'Tonight, remember, we go to concert rehearsal!'

More frequently now I was going out to concert platforms, to the excitement of the orchestra, the conductor and the audience. Leopold accompanied me and sat on one side, out of sight.

'You will be solo,' he said, 'so we practise now.' He repeated the notes on the piano. 'Play, once more, and again.' He counted and beat time. 'Play! once more!'

I thought about the rehearsal with new feelings. I thought I would speak to Madge.

Madge. I did not know her other name. Everyone called her Madge. She smiled at me often but we never had any real conversation.

She was the first violin. She was short and plump with blonde, square cut hair. Her face was white with powder. Her eyes, in puffy beds, looked sad though her hoarse voice could be heard all the time laughing and talking. Whenever I heard her voice, I had to listen. I knew every detail of her black dresses. She had three different ones. All of them shabby. She used sequins and lace, she told me later, to keep herself smart. I listened to her fragments of talk behind the flaps of music. She spoke to everyone but not to me. I knew about her from her talk, she complained about her husband, he ran his own business, she could not stand him or his business, that was how she spoke about him. Her hints of married unhappiness and her vivacious sorrow and the fact that she was many years older made her interesting and romantic.

I thought I would invite Madge to supper the following night, after the concert. How I would manage this I did not know.

Meanwhile Leopold and I went, as usual, to the hospital. The street and pavements were wet, water dripped from shining leaves. Refreshed gardens gave off exquisite scents from bushes weighed down with water drops.

Beyond the massive pillars of the porch, I stood in the cool hall tracing the inlaid flowers, a green and blue formal mosaic in marble, with the wet toe of my shoe. Palms in polished brass containers stood on either side of the reception desk. Leopold, disturbing the meditation of a solitary nun, beckoned to me. There seemed to be a peaceful order in the whiteness and the slow keys turning in well oiled locks. We made the usual journey through passages with locked doors at either end. We entered and passed through those long vaulted halls where children sat half grown in uneasy silence. We reached the brown hall where the women, in their brown dresses and headcloths, were arranged in rows on their benches.

Our singing class had not started when one of the women, with a strange cry, as if of recognition, left her place on the bench and came awkwardly towards us. Leopold rose from the piano, his face was pale, lined with concern; there was a tenderness in his expression which I could not understand. An orderly came forward at once and took hold of the woman as if to push her back to her place.

'Wait!' Leopold said. 'What is it?' he questioned in the low gentle voice I knew so well. I felt impatient, I wanted to get the class over, I waited for Leopold because I had always waited for him. The women waited too, restless, undulating on their benches.

'Let me take her back,' the orderly said, 'she'd be better . . . .'

'No wait!' Leopold looked upon the woman with kindness and patience. He seemed to look upon her with love. I tried to understand what it was she was trying to say.

'How is with Waldemar?' she gasped at length. I thought I must be mistaken, she could not have really said this. But Leopold took her gently by both arms, his exceptional hands seemed to soothe and stroke her coarse, bulky flesh. He bent his head towards her.

'All is well,' he said in a low voice. 'All is well.'

'Bring me — oh bring —' she began to sob and the words were unrecognizable and her eyes, when they looked again at Leopold, seemed to have no more recognition in them, no more knowledge of anything, they were like pale wells overflowing. She allowed herself to be taken by the orderly. Leopold watched as the young man gently led the shapeless, dejected woman away.

How Waldemar is loved I thought to myself. I wanted to ask Leopold who this woman was and ask him, straight out, if Waldemar was alive still, ask him if I had really seen him in the night or was it a dream that he was alive. Could I really be free I asked myself if I knew Waldemar was alive, hidden in that dreadful room. I was elated and tired and I took no part in the singing class, letting Leopold conduct and play all through those terrible songs we had there every week.

We walked home together and I thought I would ask Leopold about Waldemar at the next corner. The corners came and went and I could not speak. When we came near the Moreton Bay fig tree by the gate Leopold said to me to rest.

'Tonight is concert rehearsal!' he said and we went up the broken steps of the back verandah together. I thought I would spend the afternoon sorting out my life and arranging what I would do in the future. But first I wanted to find Louise and kiss her with the kiss I promised myself, alone, with no one else there. Then I would ask her the questions I wanted to ask.

No one was about in the quiet shabby house and I looked for Louise. The door to Tante Rosa's room stood open and I stepped inside. I was familiar with the plain furniture and the pictures darkly reflected in the mirror. As a boy I had often waited there for ear drops or a bandage or for Tante Rosa's favourite medicine, castor oil. The room was severe with cleanliness and order. The pictures were as meaningless for me now as they had been in my childhood. I went through this room as if in a dream. Aunt Heloise was not in her room either and beyond her glossy pink eiderdown was Louise's door. This door I opened and I looked in to the pretty room which was hers.

Penetrating the two guarding rooms I felt excited. I looked with delight at her room. It was small and framed in flowers for there were two little windows overhung with wisteria. Immediately outside were two trees grown together, the sweet scented chinese privet and a cape lilac. These were the enchantment pressing into the small maidenly room. I seemed to be trespassing. I looked with love upon all her possesions; it was the same love I had had for her when I was a boy. It gave me pleasure to look at this quiet little room where she slept safely, guarded by her aunts. She had a small writing table and a white painted chair and a neat narrow bed. On the wall was a postcard pinned up. *Kreuz im Gebirge* a painting by C.D. Friedrich 1774-1840. It was a painting of dark pines on a rock with the tiny Christ figure on the cross hanging with suffering and humility against the setting sun. I supposed she had chosen it.

I wondered if they were all upstairs with Waldemar, perhaps playing something with him to help him through the tedious hours. What game could he play now? Or perhaps they were feeding him, letting him cover himself with honey. Did he still love honey?

And then as I stood on the landing at the foot of that second staircase, I thought perhaps he was not up there at all. I was about to go up to see when Louise ran up the other staircase to find me.

'Soup Jacob,' she called, 'have your soup, it's getting cold.' And quickly I ran downstairs trying to catch her, but all I caught was her laughter as she disappeared first through one door and then another.

VII

Madge cannot stand being alone in the house with her husband. She told me so after the rehearsal when we were leaving to go home.

'He follows me about,' she complained, 'he makes stupid jokes all the time. He knows I don't love him but he won't believe it, sort of makes him self-conscious, if you know what I mean.' She had never said these things to me before. I knew from hearing her tell other people.

I had only a few minutes to talk to her. Leopold was waiting for me in the draughty passage. In spite of spending my afternoon resting and planning ways in which I could enjoy my new freedom, I felt tied into the house, joined to the people by invisible cords. It was by their acts of kindness they imprisoned me. As a boy I had only to call out in a dream and Tante Rosa was immediately beside my bed to comfort me. Leopold was devoting himself to my music lessons. And, I was, without any effort on my part, engaged to Louise. I wanted all that I had, but I wanted something else as well.

Leopold, distinguished and elderly in his dark overcoat, stood smiling and waiting for me.

'Please,' I whispered to Madge, 'let me take you to supper after the concert next week.' She looked at me in surprise.

'Well thanks very much,' she said. 'I'll be ready on the dot.' She made a little dot in the air with her forefinger, her voice was delightful, a hoarse secret whisper.

'Heard the story of the week,' I heard her saying as I held the door open for Leopold. 'Jacob's taking me out to supper Friday.' I smiled to myself. I would have to explain to Leopold, ask him not to come to the concert. However could I do this? He never missed a concert or a rehearsal. We always came together and left together. Leopold regarded the members of the orchestra as vulgar people. He told me once that some of the people just played to make a living and that they had no feeling for music at all. 'They have no ear, they have nothing except a certain skill to manipulate their fingers and an instrument and so produce the required sounds.' It was because of Leopold's attitude that I kept myself apart from the orchestra. All the same I longed sometimes to be with them and talk with them, as one of them, especially Madge. She had become for me something forbidden, and so I thought, I must have her.

I could not think how to tell Leopold not to come with me. All the week this problem was uppermost. There were several things on my mind. I still had not experimented with kissing Louise. I watched for a chance but we were never left alone together. Tante Rosa or Aunt Heloise seemed to spring from behind doors or out of cupboards, from the very floorboards, as I stepped towards the kiss. I meant too to watch the upper staircase to see if Tante Rosa carried trays of food up there or if she came down with the rosebud pail. But Leopold rewrote a cadenza and wanted me to practise it and, when at last I was free from the extra lessons and practice, there was no sign of anyone upstairs.

One afternoon I had the chance. I stepped across the square of light from the west window and went up the staircase, three steps at a time, as lightly as I could. The passage was dark and smelled as if unused for years. The door to the end room was locked. I listened but heard only the beating of my own heart.

On Friday Leopold had severe pain in his varicosed leg and Aunt Heloise begged him to lie down but he insisted on playing for my cello practice. Afterwards he went to hospital as usual. I went with him and searched, from my place beside the piano, among the expressionless faces for the woman who had cried for Waldemar. Leopold conducted the singing class as though there had been nothing unusual last time.

In the afternoon he was forced to lie down and Aunt Heloise ran to and fro with cold compresses. By evening he was no better.

'Good luck to the Prince of the Cello,' he called to me. I bowed to him from the door. I was exquisitely dressed in a suit of expensive cloth and I was at ease at last about the evening. Tante Rosa and Aunt Heloise and Louise were grouped around Leopold attending to him. Later, I knew they would be dispersed to perform the mysterious tasks of the evening. Louise had a student coming. She came with me to the door.

'Now that we are engaged,' I said tenderly to her. 'And now that I am rich there is no need for you to teach.' She looked at me.

'Perhaps Aunt Heloise could give up her dressmaking?' she whispered. 'Perhaps you could tell her that.' she said.

'No need for either, teaching or dressmaking,' I said proudly. It seemed that money lay in heaps on all sides of me. I had only to reach out a hand.

'No need for either,' I put out my hand and gathered up some red velvet which lay over a chair in the hall, I tossed the soft folds of the velvet as if disturbing a rich pile of money.

'Oh don't,' Louise exclaimed. 'It is all tacked! Aunt Heloise was all night pinning and tacking the seams, it's all done with tissue paper between.' Carefully she smoothed out my extravagant gesture. She was always so careful for her aunts.

'Tell Aunt Heloise—' I began and then I thought of the kiss. 'Louise!' I leaned towards her and my mouth twitched. I turned my head and buried my kiss in the collar of her dress.

On the way to the concert, alone, I breathed in the fresh air of my freedom. Louise should go out more I thought, but of course we could not go alone. In my present exultation I shrank from taking Tante Rosa and Aunt Heloise to a restaurant, even if I dared to go in one myself. I could imagine them feeling the cloth of the waiter's jacket, between knowledgeable thumb and forefinger assessing its quality, or sniffing at the innocence of some dish and putting it aside saying, *Das schmecht mir nicht!*

Before the concert I missed Leopold, I was accustomed to having him near, out of sight, but near. My watchfulness during the week had made me tired and nervous. I had been listening for sounds which would prove Waldemar was in the house. I had been listening for his dreadful laugh and for the curious way in which he spoke when his teeth on the food encrusted wire were not in his mouth. I had been watching Leopold too to see if he would reveal something about the crying woman at the hospital.

I looked for Madge and, across the restless preparation of the orchestra, we smiled at one another.

Then I played my cello. The music seemed to go on for ever and yet was over all too soon.

At last I stepped with Madge on to the pavement outside, beside Madge, alone at last, I realised I had no money with me.

'Well here's a how d'you do!' she said and laughed. 'My escort has no money!' she said. There was no scorn in her voice. 'And what's more,' she said, 'neither have I!' We stood still, I nearly wept with rage and shame. I was trembling after the performance, Haydn's cello concerto always affected me profoundly. I remembered so clearly my wallet on the table in my room. I wondered, madly, whether to go back there and creep into the quiet dark house and fetch it and come out again to Madge. But they had a habit of being all around me straight away with their sweet wine and little milk biscuits, pressing me with their crochetted cushions and soft voices to give me rest after playing.

Oh sorry! Sorry Madge!'

Madge squeezed my arm. She had enough for the bus fare. I let her take me on the bus away from all the noise and the fashionable places, one of which I had, in my mind, dared to enter with her.

It occurred to me as we entered her house, a little brick place with flat windows and a front door which opened straight into the sitting-room, I did not even know her other name. Everyone called her Madge. She had stiff blonde hair and grey eyes, puffy underneath, and a full mouth. Apart from these details and the knowledge that she found her husband unbearable I knew nothing about her at all.

'How do you like my hair tonight?' she asked as she switched on the light.

'Oh very nice,' I said. I was used to admiring hair but hers was different.

'It's a hyacinth rinse,' she whispered and she bent her head. I leaned over and inhaled the fragrance of her blue hair.

The room was very small, a sofa, Madge referred to it as a studio couch, and two chairs were placed at right angles on a manure coloured carpet. Over the fireplace which had a closed stove in it was an oval mirror. On tiptoe Madge examined her face and hair in the mirror. From the mirror her grey eyes, slits in their puffy beds, looked at me wickedly.

'Where is he?' I was uneasy.

'In bed of course, silly!' she kicked off her shoes. 'I'll fix a sandwich,' she said, 'but first I'll have to get rid of this.' Twisting her body from side to side, performing some extraordinary movements, she reached under her skirt and

60

unfastened her suspenders and brought out, from its accustomed place, a garment which, with a whip-like movement, she flung behind the door.

'God!' she said, 'that's better! I don't want to burn my bra but I wouldn't mind setting fire to that thing. I can have a good scratch now.' She unclipped her ear-rings and put them on the ugly mantelpiece.

'My bladder's up to my chin,' she said and went out of the room quickly.

There was nothing in the room for me to look at so I investigated with interest her little tossed off, warm, perfumed corset. And I listened uneasily for the husband to come.

She came back with a tray and we ate hungrily, half opposite each other, knees touching knees, on the sofa which she kept calling a studio couch. I was shivering so she switched on a little electric heater and the warmth was comforting.

'Have some more plonk,' she said and I did not know what she meant. 'The wine,' she said. 'It's cheap stuff.' I told her about my father and about Uncle Otto and the vineyard. I tried to explain about the barrels and the vines and the quality of the grapes and about my mother, who never learnt to speak English, and about her standing in her black dress in among the yellowing leaves of the vines in the middle of the long sunny afternoon. Madge listened to me eagerly.

'Funny,' she said in her husky voice. 'It was always sunshine when I was a kid too,' she paused. 'Must be the wine talking!' she said and laughed. I tried to tell her something of my lifewith Leopold and Tante Rosa and Aunt Heloise.

'But I am dull!' I said to her.

'I could listen to your voice for ever,' she said, 'that's why I keep asking you about them.' She put her head back to where my arm was resting along the back of the studio couch. Her neck was ripe and smooth and beautiful and I wanted to get up and kneel to this beauty. I hardly knew her and I wanted to know her more and, at the same time, to keep reverence by restraint. She moved a little closer to me, and we sat together for some time.

'I must really be going home,' I looked at my watch. 'I am keeping you from going to bed.' Madge laughed as I stood up politely.

'Oh you are a Funny One,' she said, 'But I love your good manners.' I was not sure if she was mocking me and this together with the fear that her husband might appear made me feel uneasy. She put her hand on my arm as if to detain me.

'But really I must go,' I insisted.

On the way home I felt relieved that I had not talked about Waldemar and especially that I had not spoken of Louise. She was something apart from the way in which I had spent these two hours. My mouth tasted of the wine and the pickle sauce which Madge had spread in the sandwiches. When I held my hand to my face I could faintly smell the perfume she used.

'Welcome at last to the Prince of the Cello,' Leopold called out softly as I came in. They were all waiting up for me with the sweet wine and the little milk biscuits on the cream lace table cloth. Leopold looked white and drawn, I supposed it was the pain in his legs.

'I was invited —' I began my apology to the large dim room. Louise came quickly to my side.

'Explain to Tante Rosa and Aunt Heloise,' she whispered. 'Tell them everything is all right, they have been so worried over you.' So I began to explain and they gently nodded their heads and gave me biscuits and wine and I sat beside Leopold and watched Aunt Heloise wring out the folded squares of smooth, wet linen before applying them to his swollen useless legs.

VIII

Because of Leopold's illness, my life changed. He was no longer able to accompany me and I went out alone without any of them knowing where I was. I took less interest in the household. I no longer prowled about trying to discover what secret tasks were performed behind my back, or whether Waldemar was really in the house or not. I took part in a series of concerts without Leopold sitting out of sight at the edge of the orchestra. And I saw Madge more and more.

Madge took the car from her husband on Thursdays even though their living depended on his having the car. It was her day for having her hair done. One Thursday she waited for me at the end of the street and we went off together. The world unfolded in a bluish mist. The river was smooth and ice blue. The far bank looked peaceful in the sunshine, its remote flatness reaching back to where the hills were still hidden behind the flimsy curtains of the morning. It was like having a picture postcard of tremendous size alongside. It seemed as if I were seeing the roads and the river and the hills for the first time in my life. I breathed deeply, excited by the scent left by that private hour of intimacy with the hairdresser.

'It's not so far now,' Madge said, her gloved hands competently on the steering wheel. 'We are coming up to the plantation.'

'I'd like to walk in there,' I said, looking out into the pale mist between the black, thin trunks of the pines. 'It would be lovely to walk in there, it's beautiful.' The sun was shining through the mist.

'It's only nice because you don't know it,' Madge said. 'You think it's nice. Intellectually you like it,' she grinned at me, 'you'd find it very rough underfoot and you'd get lost in no time. Just you wait for where I'm taking you.'

The plantation went on for miles and at last we came to a place where the river we had crossed and recrossed widened into an estuary. Beyond was the sea. Madge turned on to a track which led to the river's edge where there were a few holiday cottages, painted and dotted like dolls' houses in the ragged fringes of the wide, cold, shining estuary.

'Hell's Bells!' Madge cursed the potholes. Dark birds flew low over the water and the sky came down to the sea, strangely near and threatening.

'Welcome to "Sans Souci",' Madge said. She skidded in a half circle on the sand in front of a little pink house. Quickly she skipped up the wooden steps and unlocked the door and quickly I followed. She opened windows, talking happily, telling me the rooms in turn. She plunged into a cupboard and brought out an armful of clothes, and taking off her neat blue costume, she put on a striped shirt and some old trousers and, standing with bare feet, buttoned the shirt and carefully tied her hair into a coloured scarf.

I was relieved she was not going to be in stockinged feet. Something about her feet, flirtatious in the trailing stockings, had been ugly and pathetic that first evening at her house.

Afterwards, the dejected stockings were what I remembered most.

'I'm cold!' I shivered. 'I'm afraid of catching cold. I get cold easily,' I said. I could not control my shivering.

'Put this on.' She handed me a rough jersey.

'Your husband's?' I asked. 'Is this his?' I took the garment with distaste. I felt ashamed to be shaking and cold.

'No it's mine,' she said. As I pulled it over my head, it smelt unmistakeably of her.

'Now we're both Madge,' I said.

'Oh Jackyboy!' Madge laughed. 'Not quite,' she said and she pressed herself against me and kissed me. She had to pull me down to her mouth. Then I kissed her as if I had known how to kiss all my life. Her eyes shone and I looked into them with delight.

'Now we are nearly,' she said.

She seemed happy and full of youth and movement, almost too much for the small rooms of the house. She sang and filled the kettle to make tea for us. She had sandwiches but neither of us wanted to eat.

'We come here a lot on weekends,' Madge said. 'It means a lot to my husband, having this place; he likes fishing.'

Perhaps she did not find him tiresome when they came here, I thought. She seemed lighthearted now with me. I had never seen her so pretty. She was very attractive, and every time she kissed me, I responded with a depth of feeling which was pleasant but disturbing.

The little hut was clean inside but shabby. We were soon warm in there and Mage explained her husband wanted it like a boat, 'that is why the windows are round,' she said. We sat close together, kissing, talking only during moments between the kisses.

Later we walked along the narrow strip of shore beyond the hut. Theirs was the last one, it stood alone in the mournful shelter of some Norfolk pines. The grassy flats broke and crumbled in tiny uneven cliffs all along the edge of the sand. We walked slowly on the sand which was hard and wet, lined with froth and bubbles of seaweed, shining green reflecting the overcast sky. The little choppy waves, all along the shore, came running in with a repetition and a noise and an unseen force and fell back all along the shore with a series of thin sighs. Madge thought she heard a frog and we stood still to try to hear it but the waves made too much noise.

'There it is again,' Madge said, but I could not hear it though it seemed she wanted me to hear it. We were holding hands. I loved her hand, the palm of her hand seemed to speak to mine. She reminded me of the deep sustained note of the cello. She seemed experienced, grief laden and yet, with quiet joy, waiting to be explored. She seemed able to be happy in the moments when we kissed each other. As we stood on the quiet shore I wanted to kiss her again and follow the kiss with a deep look into her eyes to see what expression was there but I could not.

'How old are you Madge?' I wanted to ask her, but her age did not really matter. Twenty years, thirty years what did years matter.

When we walked back the wind was suddenly colder and there was an unspoken sense of foreboding, a running out of our time together before we had had the time. The hours we had stolen were now being stolen from us. It was time to be going back.

'So you're going steady' Madge said. Facing the wind, I had begun to talk of Louise. 'So you're going steady,' she said again.

'I am betrothed to Louise since I am eighteen,' I said quietly.

'Betrothed, what a funny way to talk.'

I shrugged, 'Our language is like this; we are all foreigners,' and I tried to explain something about them. 'Tante Rosa, she is the Grenadier, very clean, she knows everything, Aunt Heloise is very fat. It is because of Tante Rosa that I pass all my exams. Leopold you have seen often, he is the finest music teacher in the world.'

'There's more to the world than your world Jackyboy,'

Madge said, 'and there's music teachers and music teachers just like there's orchestras and orchestras,' she seemed to be looking out across the wide estuary. I tried to tell her about the big old house, the endless practising, the cleaning, the evenings of music and I tried to tell her of the devotion.

'You must come and try Aunt Heloise's pâté,' I said trying to be cheerful, I was afraid again of catching cold but did not want Madge to know I was afraid. I tried to describe Louise, 'She is small and dark and her mouth is serious,' I said, 'and ever since I was fourteen I have worn a ring made from her hair.' I wished at once I had not said this, for Madge burst out laughing in a voice so unlike hers I thought someone else was there laughing.

'I like the look of Leopold,' she said, 'but the others sound really awful!' She threw a handful of seaweed into the water.

'Where do they wear their skirts?' she asked. I did not know what she meant.

'I don't know about their skirts,' I replied. 'But I know I must never hurt them because all my life they have loved me and looked after me. They have made me what I am,' I said holding up my head and looking at her.

'Oh Oh,' Madge said, 'What are you! Oh. What are you!'

Madge packed up her things, quickly, rinsing the cups we had used. She changed her clothes. I shivered in my thin jacket after the warm pullover. We drove home in the shabby car.

'Are you thinking of your husband?' I asked her. The back of the car was filled with his boxes and packets and the car smelled of these things.

'God! You'd never guess what I'm thinking,' Madge said and her eyes seemed to disappear in their puffy beds. She relapsed into a silent watchfulness of the wet road. At the end of my street she stopped for me to get out at exactly the same place where she had stopped earlier to take me.

'I don't think we better meet any more,' she said. It did not seem to me that she spoke unkindly only with a sadness which made me want to cry and run after the car as she drove off.

I walked along the pavement as if I had a stone in my heart.

I went straight upstairs to my room though I knew they would be waiting for me. When I walked about in my room something on the chest wobbled tap tapping gently as I walked to and fro, tap tapping. It was like Tante Rosa and Aunt Heloise nodding their heads from their chairs on the far side of the room whenever I came in to tell Leopold I had returned. Usually I went straight in to greet him and answer his 'How is the Prince of a Fellow?' This time I prowled about in my room. I wanted to write to Madge at once to tell her all that was piled up in my heart for her. I felt torn over her and I could not bear to recall the sadness in her voice and look.

I went to Tante Rosa's room to fetch some paper. She kept it and the envelopes on her little writing desk. Everyone who wanted writing paper fetched it from Tante Rosa's room. Of course I knew I should now have my own and I resolved to buy some. Now that I had money and my own cheque book, what difficulties were there? Tante Rosa was not in her room, she hardly ever was there. I took some sheets of the paper and an envelope and a stamp. As I turned from the modest writing table I saw, behind the door, an enormous tin of honey and Waldemar's honey jar all in a mess on some pieces of newspaper. My letter to Madge was more important and I hurried along to my own room.

'I just want to write,' I explained to Tante Rosa who appeared at the head of the stairs as I crossed the landing.

'Of course Jacob,' she smiled her gracious severe smile. 'Come soon, we are all waiting for you.'

They were all waiting for me, it was always like this. All of them waiting for me. I could not write with the feeling of the household waiting for me, so I combed my hair and changed into a fresh shirt and went to them. I was very hungry after my day.

Strange preparations had been made. They had rearranged the big room where we always were together, as if for visitors. And there were two visitors there; the room and the company seemed to sparkle suddenly into life as I entered the room as if in anticipation of some festivities.

'Welcome to a Prince of a Fellow!' Leopold called from his chaise-longue and the two guests rose and came forward with Tante Rosa and Aunt Heloise, both of whom wore their best blouses. Dr Horowizc greeted me, kissing me on both cheeks, and the priest took both my hands in his and murmured words I was unable to hear. I strained as if in a deep dream to hear what he said, but his voice was low and he kept his head bent down.

The room was prepared as if for a banquet. The large table was spread with a white cloth, and all the silver and glass, freshly polished, was laid upon it, seven places were set and on the sideboard were several covered dishes, and a wedding cake tied with a white silk ribbon was on the low lace covered table. Little bowls of frangipani stood round the cake. Pink hydrangeas, out of season, and dipped for refreshment all day in water, wept as if to relieve the heaviness of their heads.

In the fragrance of frangipani Louise, strangely and beautifully dressed all in white and with her face veiled, came towards me and we were married.

Was I waking? Was I dreaming? Of course I remembered I was supposed to marry Louise. It had been arranged that day I became the owner of my father's land.

I was a bird in a snake's eye. I had never thought it could be avoided. If I thought anything, it was, 'Not yet. Not yet.'

This afternoon I had been on the point of merging into Madge, but now I was married. To Louise.

There was a poem Tante Rosa had once tried to teach me. In her monotonous, clear but inaccurate English, with the stresses falling equally on each syllable, it did not sound musical as a poem should. All I could remember was that it was about a dove which had been precious to a girl but which had died. Perhaps it had been tied too tightly with a thread of the girl's own hair.

The day spent on the shore of the quiet estuary faded and was absorbed into the fragrance and the familiar conversation of the soft agreeing voices. The words of the marriage and the priest's blessing hovered over the passing of the dishes of food. I poured wine for the guests and I remembered later thanking Leopold and Tante Rosa and Aunt Heloise for my sweet and lovely bride.

'Bravo!' my father-in-law called from the long chair. I kissed Tante Rosa's elderly cheek and was surprised at the softness and the fragrance.

'We love you so much,' Aunt Heloise whispered when I bent to brush her heavily rouged cheek with my lips. 'Especially Leopold loves you.'

'I am deeply touched,' I replied.

Louise peeled grapes for me and we ate glacé fruits sparkling in edible silver. We cut the wedding cake; the knife had a porcelain handle decorated with rosebuds. I had never seen it before. I realised that the many treasures, the tablecloth and the candlesticks and the silver dishes, must have been brought out from hidden trunks and boxes. I had never seen them before.

'Dance Prince, dance!' my father-in-law called. Aunt Heloise sat at the piano and played the Fandango from Mozart's 'Don Giovanni.' The imitation gold in her blouse rippled and flashed on her bosom. I knew one had to dance at weddings. I bowed to Louise.

'Take Tante Rosa first,' she whispered, hardly lifting her eyelids. So I danced with Tante Rosa. Then she played while I danced with Aunt Heloise, round and round the big room. My father-in-law applauded every time we passed his chair, Dr Horowizc and Father Basil Francis remained behind the scattered battlements of dishes on the other side of the white tablecloth. As I danced it seemed as if they sat grey and asleep in their chairs. I looked at Louise thinking I would soon have her to myself. She sat quite still, all in white, waiting.

Something of the day remained; it was an unnameable desire and I longed to dance with Louise and dance her out of the room. But each time as I circled the room, and in my mind flew with Louise to the heavily curtained door, I wanted to step through it with someone else. Very faintly my hands smelled still of Madge. It was of her I was thinking.

Then I danced with Louise.

'Do you remember when you first came?' she whispered. 'I have loved you since that day,' she kept her eyes down as she spoke and her voice was low. 'Did you know,' she whispered, 'the first man a woman loves she loves always and for ever.'

'I am the first?' She kept her face turned down. 'I am the first?' I asked again. 'Look up at me,' I said. As we passed Leopold we turned our heads to smile as he clapped gently.

'Look at me,' I begged her to look. If she would look for one moment so that we could know each others' eyes perhaps everything could be changed.

Round and round the large room we went on dancing passing the arm chairs, the white table cloth, the chaise-longue and the piano. In turn as we danced, we nodded slightly to Tante Rosa, to Aunt Heloise, to the sleeping guests and to Leopold. The piano pleaded under Tante Rosa's hands.

It was as if we were children again.

'Would you like to marry me one day?'

'Perhaps.'

'Only perhaps? Oh Jacob!'

'I do want to marry you if you'll have me.'

Here now was this almost expected event. Ever since those days this had been expected. That I should one day be a married man had naturally occurred to me. But even after the surprise celebration of our engagement, on the day of my inheritance, the idea of marriage had seemed remote, something vague, talked about in laughter while eating apples and trying on rings made from human hair, something looked forward to from childhood but, like a disease experienced by adults, never reached.

Once more round the room nodding and smiling to the chairs. Since this wedding had been arranged in the appalling strength of apparent devotion, I felt something must be done to enable me, in spite of the invisible, inescapable power drawing me deeper into the household, to make some kind of re-entry of my own. I wanted to start my married life with my own feelings.

'Look at me,' I asked her once more.

'I can't,' she whispered. 'I am going to faint.' I kissed her so that all might see, gently on her hair as she was fainting.

Dr Horowizc prescribed a rest for Louise and she went with her two aunts to the room which, unknown to me till then, had been prepared for our wedding night.

Leopold asked me to fetch my cello which I did and, after our two guests had gone, I practised the slow movement of the Haydn cello concerto. He lay with his eyes closed and gently beat time for me and the long sustained notes filled the room and hovered, holding back an exquisite pain, over the remains of the white wedding feast.

IX

I went straight to my own room, elated and yet trembling with the agitation I felt immediately after playing the cello. I walked to and fro in the small space of my room. The tiny tapping thing wobbled and tapped on the chest of drawers. I took out my cello again fondling the instrument tenderly as I did so. I played the opening phrases of the cello concerto as if for Madge, as I would play it for her on the next concert evening.

'. . . I am like a horse galloping without a rider,' I wrote to Madge, 'after we have kissed each other as we have, I must see you again. Please see me again. I cannot live like this. I am so sad when I know you are sad. Without you I am not anything.' and I signed myself 'Jackyboy' which was her name for me.

I went down in the quiet house to go out to post my letter. Tante Rosa was crossing the hall.

'I am just going out to the post,' I said to her.

'Of course Jacob.'

I knew she would not stop me or even ask about the letter. She stood aside to let me go to the door and I knew she would quietly appear again later to close and bolt the door for the night at whatever time I chose to come back.

Restlessly I paced about in my narrow room. The night air was fragrant with the night scented things, the jasmine and the bells of the datura. To and fro, turning after two steps like an animal in a cage, to and fro. I was thinking of Madge and aching over her last words. I thought she might be sitting somewhere, near her husband yet alone in her unhappiness. I thought too about the clean, new room where Louise was also alone, on her wedding night. Alone in the big white bed.

The thing wobbled and tapped on the chest every time I creaked over the floor boards, just a tiny tap tap, I looked there to see what it was. I saw at once that it was that grotesque piece of battered jewellery, Waldemar's two false teeth on their crooked, dislocated wire. Here in my room.

I thought he might have put them there himself and this frightened me especially as it seemed that they were bigger than the ones he had all those years ago. It was as if he had come like a monster from his lair at the top of the house, an animal escaping with the intention of doing some unknown evil thing. I tried to tell myself that Tante Rosa, taking the teeth to clean them, had in the distractions of the busy day, forgotten them. All the same I was frightened and, in my fear, I went along the passage and into the bridal bedroom. In among the unknown drapery I was a stranger. Colliding with my own image because of the unaccustomed placing of a wardrobe with its long, coffined mirrors facing the door, I cried out and groped towards the large, high bed with blood streaming from my nose.

My cry brought Tante Rosa and Aunt Heloise in their familiar night clothes, their soft voices echoing in the night.

'Did you call Jacob?' Tante Rosa asked and, as if with

relief, they went for basins of cold water and clean soft rags. I sat up on the bed beside Louise, spotting the sheets with my bright blood and allowing Aunt Heloise to press the folded, cold cloths on the back of my neck.

When the bleeding had stopped and we were at last alone Louise lay down.

'I am so tired,' she said and smiled at me. I slid off the bed and crouched beside her and held her hand to my lips.

'Go to sleep Louise,' I said to her. 'I will stay here and watch beside you.' At once my knees began to ache but I wanted to please her, to show my devotion in some way.

'Get undressed and come to bed,' Louise said. 'We are supposed. It is all right, we are husband and wife, it is expected.'

Quickly I undressed and it seemed to me to be the most comfortable bed I had ever had. I was swallowed up in the softness. The well laundered sheets possessed a dream-like quality of repose. In this soft warmth I reached for her hand and pressed it. The hand was rough with work, it was small and childish.

'I love you so much Jacob,' she said and put her arms round me. 'Do you know that whenever I changed your sheets I put them on to my bed because when I slept in them after you had slept in them I was near to you.' She stretched herself beside me. 'I used to stretch out in the sheets to have as much of them touch me as possible.'

'Louise,' I whispered. 'I can hardly believe it.'

'Do you love me Jacob?'

'Of course.'

'Then show me.'

I felt the longing in her body. I kissed her and wanted to please her but my trembling body failed us both. I bit my pillow in shame. I saw her wide-awake eyes overflowing with disappointment in the darkness. I must have fallen asleep straight away for I thought of nothing except that I was dreadfully tired too.

Madge was too generous not to answer my note. I knew this, but no answer came and I was afraid something might have happened to her. On Friday she was not at the concert. I played as if for her even though she was not there. I played the cadenza brilliantly. I played as I wanted to love, delicately and with understanding, with restraint and yet with power. As I played I closed by eyes and the long thoughtful notes sustained me in my love and I gave myself up to the music. Cello.

I longed more than ever to see Madge. Perhaps her husband had seen my note and had locked her in her bedroom. Or was it only in the house where I had been brought up that things like this could be done. Only from devotion, this locking in.

After the concert I wanted to see Madge. I tried not to think of them all waiting for me in that large, dimly lit room where the curtains made mysterious boundaries and the aunts chose chairs which were far away, pushed back into the corners so that, when they spoke, their voices were like soft waves running up a shallow beach. In my mind I could hear their voices, like waves, running up and falling back and running up and falling back. My father-in-law would be waiting too with the draughts set out beside his swollen legs. On the table between Tante Rosa and Aunt Heloise the lace covered plate of sterile milk biscuits would wait too for my return.

Louise would be waiting for me. What else had she to do? I knew a great deal more about Louise and, at the same time, I knew nothing. Every night I was able to look upon her soft young body, to see the white skin of her small breasts, to trace lightly, with my finger, the delicate pattern of fine blue veins just beneath the skin. Every night I could pay homage with reverence, I could renew my promise to myself that never again would I do anything which would hurt Louise. Now after the concert I refused to think of them. I thought only of going to see Madge. Everything seemed to turn towards Madge and I hurried towards the bus terminus.

Crowds of people were on the pavement, the audience, mainly, pouring from the well lit foyer. In the crowd I felt strange and lonely like a sick man who has left his bed when he should have stayed in it. I pushed my way through the well-dressed pressing of the well-mannered groups of people.

And then I saw Madge.

A man was helping her to cross the busy street, his hand beneath her elbow, his whole body leaning, with care, towards her. He helped her into a car and tucked a rug all round her.

'So she heard me play the cello concerto after all,' I felt elated and pleased and remembered again the second movement which seems to speak of human tenderness and expectation and perhaps even of explanation and reason.

I wondered why Madge should have been in the audience instead of on the platform. The car turned in the road, in spite of the stream of traffic, and drew up alongside.

'It was beautiful!' Madge said to me in a hoarse voice as she rolled down the window. 'Jacob, I want you to meet my Better Half.' So I bent down, bowing to the car and he ducked his head to be able to say,

'How's things!'

I was unable to make out his face apart from the long, sad lines of it. He seemed a dejected man in spite of his best clothes and in spite of knowing and possessing the most desirable woman. I had already seen something of the inviting loveliness of Madge, her strong throat and neck were indicative of what I had not yet seen. Suddenly, standing in the street, I suffered a terrible choking sensation of hatred directed towards this man who was quite innocent of doing anything wrong or unkind to me. He simply had the misfortune of possessing every night of his life the warmth and vitality and the generosity of this woman.

'It was lovely. Really, the cello,' Madge said.

'Can we drop you home?' the husband asked.

'Oh no, really no! It is out of your way, it is all right.'

'Aw come on!' Madge said. 'It's not far, get in!' Her husband leaned behind her and opened the door, pulling some of his boxes and packages along the back seat to make room for me. The movement of the door opening was compelling.

So we drove all three together. There was a fragrance in the car, a mixture of her perfume and the worn upholstery upon which her warm body sat, it made me feel bold and able to make an intimate remark.

'I was on my way to see what had happened to you,' I said.

'Bad cold!' Madge said, and I noticed again her voice, which was usually hoarse was much more so.

'Didn't the others tell you at rehearsal?'

Of course I hadn't asked anyone where Madge was. Only I missed her terribly, staying the shortest time with the orchestra, going off restlessly, wondering about her.

'I've been drinking cold water all day,' Madge said. 'Not like me at all. If I drink water it's a sign I'm ill,' she said.

The old car went softly through the streets.

'Honey?' Madge asked her husband, 'could you get me some of my lozenges at the All Night Chemist?' Clever Madge to lengthen our time together and for a few moments we were alone.

I leaned into her fur collar, breathing her in greedily. 'Oh Madge! Why didn't you write to me?' I asked in a low voice.

'I am afraid,' Madge replied.

'Of what?' There was a little pause of sadness. 'Oh. Of what?' My feeling of tenderness was indescribable.

'Myself,' she whispered. It was the sweetest confession.

'Don't be afraid,' I comforted her. Quickly I pushed my face beyond the soft fur collar to her warm neck and with my lips caressed the smooth skin and she moaned just a tiny moan, enough for me to hear.

'Oh Jacob!'

'Madge!'

I wished her husband need never come back.

'You should buy yourself a vehicle,' Madge said to me

78

lightly as her husband dropped a package into her lap, as if we had been discussing transport in his absence.

'Tell you what,' Madge said in the deep, black shadow of the Moreton Bay tree by my gate, 'How about we all go to the hut for the weekend. You and Louise and us two,' she said and her eyes were suddenly sparkling behind the stupid bit of veil she wore tied over the front of her hat.

'Thank you very much,' I replied with the stiff good manners of my upbringing. From the pavement I made a small bow.

'We'll fetch you about noon. We'll go rough, nothing elaborate.' Madge spoke in that light tone which I was not sure about. I wondered if it was unhappiness which changed her voice. When she laughed I was not sure of her sincerity.

'We'll rough it!' she cried. In the light of the street lamp it seemed she had eyes like a cat, behind the tiny spots of the veil, they were brimming amber as if about to shed tears of coloured glass.

'Thank you. Thank you very much,' I said and walked beneath the big tree into the darkness of the night to the blackness which was the house waiting for me.

I took with me into the house the memory of the tiny gold pin I had seen on a narrow black ribbon on Madge's creamy shoulder. I smiled as I thought of it and my hand, when I put it to my face, breathed her perfume back to me. Holding my breath to keep this sensual fragrance I stepped into the large, dim room where they were waiting.

'Good evening to a Prince of a Fellow,' my father-in-law held out both hands to me. The aunts came from the corners of the room and were quickly busy about the little table on which were the plates of pale biscuits, a flask of sweet wine and some glasses.

'Eat Tante Rosa's biscuit,' whispered Louise to me. 'She has tried a special recipe today.' So I ate from the Grenadier's plate. As I drank the wine Aunt Heloise poured for me I seemed to look at Tante Rosa for the first time in all the years I had lived under her care. I took a second biscuit from the plate she offered and, for a moment our eyes met;

I saw in hers a depth of deep brown like a dark pool of sadness and an expression which made me feel suddenly cold for I realised, for the first time, that Tante Rosa hated me. All the time she had offered me food and had watched me eating and had hated me.

Shaking under the hovering shadow of Tante Rosa I sat down beside my father-in-law.

'Now you have money you must travel,' he said. I thought of wind and rain and waves and the boredom of the ship's rail moving above the horizon and below the horizon. I thought of the mysterious knowledge which takes a ship across so many miles of sea faultlessly. I thought of wharves and customs' sheds and railway yards and strange people and unknown language. I felt an excitement at the thought of seeing and knowing new things previously only told about or read of in the books Leopold had.

'You must study in Vienna,' Leopold was saying. And I thought of music and I thought of Madge and I knew I could not leave. I smiled to myself remembering the little gold pin. I could not go away from Madge. As I looked across at Louise I knew I could not leave Madge and I smiled at Louise with all the tenderness I was feeling for Madge and said, 'I will not leave Louise,' and it seemed to me she looked at me in a way I was not able to understand.

I told them then of the invitation.

'So!' Leopold said. 'They invite you, they are good people. He, the husband waits for her while she plays. It is her work to play. He waits as I waited for you Prince.' My father-in-law said, 'He is a good fellow. He has a face exactly like our old coachman back home, a good fellow, an excellent fellow, nonetheless, but a coachman all the same. Our coachman! His feet were so big,' my father-in-law laughed, remembering, 'that he had to get out of bed to turn over.'

'In those little holiday cottages, one has to be so careful,' Aunt Heloise said, lowering her voice till she was hardly audible, 'The walls are so thin, you know,' she said to Louise. 'Remember, always put one hand behind the toilet roll while you use it otherwise the whole house can hear the fixture turning. Is that not so Rosa?' Heloise appealed to Tante Rosa who acknowledged the advice with a single nod of her head.

'Remember Rosa, that place in the Alps so many years ago!' and Tante Rosa and Aunt Heloise nodded and murmured as if they were turning over the pages of an old photograph album together. Louise whispered to me to say something nice about Tante Rosa's hair as Heloise had dressed it this evening for her. I trembled as I paid my compliment, Tante Rosa thanked me and I avoided her eyes.

Later in my narrow room I tried to recapture from my jacket sleeve the faint fragrance. I wanted to know and have everything of Madge.

I only knew it from music and from books and I wanted it now from Madge. And as I lay on my bed dreaming I thought that Madge was right, I should have a car of my own. There was no reason why I should not have one, something expensive and beautiful and Madge should drive it whenever she wanted to. And later, much later, it was almost dawn, I went softly to the bed where my wife lay and at once I fell deeply asleep.

X

I began to see Louise more clearly. She knew nothing about modern things and had a slight odour of the body which, together with the lavender soap she used, gave her a kind of distinction. In the morning I went out and bought things for her, deodorant, talcum powder and perfume.

'This you rub under your arms,' I explained showing her the things I had been choosing for her, 'and this you sprinkle all over your body and just a little of this behind your ears.'

Obediently she packed them into the small bag she was preparing for us to take to the hut. She did not ask how I had learned about them.

Madge said later she was flattered that I had bought for Louise the same perfume she had. We had a moment of time alone and Madge tried to take my hand but I moved away. I could see that it hurt her but it was enough to bring Louise out to a strange place with strange people and I wanted to be careful to protect her.

'How do you know? I asked softly.

'She showed me as soon as we arrived here, the presents she had from you this morning,' Madge said. 'It really touched me,' she said, 'to see you chose the same for her as I have, exactly!' she spoke lightly. I was burdened because of hurting her, not letting our hands touch and stepping back away from her. I thought I heard Louise on the wooden steps outside. She had gone out to look at the noisy sea birds.

Louise came in delighted with the hungry gulls and we both looked fondly at her. Madge put her hand on Louise, on her head and shoulder.

'Your hair is quite damp,' she said. 'Don't get cold here or Jacob'll kill me!'

Madge's husband was bringing things in from the car, the charity flag of the Blind Society on its little white walking stick reminiscent on his coat lapel of the morning in the suburban shopping centre. He came in laden with cardboard boxes of provisions.

'Did you remember the duck?' Madge asked him as he stepped indoors. Yes he had remembered everything, he even quacked and pretended to walk like a duck. He burrowed into the shopping. Louise wanted to take some bread out to the birds.

'It's so cold,' Madge said, 'out there.' She paused in the putting away of the groceries. 'You finish these Norm,' she said to her husband. And rather than be alone in the little kitchen with this man with whom I could see no possibilities of making any kind of relationship, I walked outside into the cold dampness and followed the two women along the shore.

Madge had snatched up a black silk scarf. I watched as she draped it, a foolish little shroud, over Louise's head. It would be useless against the cold. I tried to warn them about the cold. The wind coming, as it did, over the wide estuary brought the cold air from the water. My voice was lost in the screaming of the gulls as they circled hungrily swooping for the bits of bread.

Madge and Louise walked on together along the strip of wet sand. I wondered what kind of a time we would all have together in this remote spot and in the small hut. I thought I had been stupid to accept the invitation and even more stupid to bring Louise. I wished that Louise and Madge would be friends. Friendship between them, I thought, would make my own position more simple and perhaps take the light tone of insincerity out of Madge's voice. If Madge could love Louise and know all her qualities, then I could love them both. I liked Madge best when her voice was hoarse, it reminded me of the times she whispered to me at rehearsals. It was at once intimate and revealing, the sound of her real voice.

As before, the little waves came steadily chopping up the shore, falling back with a faint sighing beside me as I walked shivering and wishing to be indoors.

I was worried because I had not had a chance to tell Madge that Louise and I were now married. She would hardly be able to understand the way in which things were done in that house. So far the sleeping arrangements had not been discussed. We had taken the little hut by surprise, coming suddenly upon its huddled quietness, the four of us with the cartons of food and our baggage stuffed in the old car. We seemed to wake the hut from a shivery sleep as we opened the door and spread ourselves in the tiny rooms. Norman in particular, important with the mysterious duties of the householder, was busy immediately. I stood by the window taking no part in the resuscitation of the house. I was used to being apart, my time was spent in being apart, playing the cello or prowling about the big, old house searching for some kind of explanation.

As I walked behind Louise and Madge, I realised Louise must have shown Madge the presents I had given her as soon as we were in the hut. This thought touched and pleased me.

When I went to buy the things for Louise I left the house

84

early, during all the scrubbing and cleaning and tidying time. I bought chocolates for Tante Rosa and Aunt Heloise and for Louise too in case she might be annoyed at my other presents.

They were pleased with the gifts. Louise opened hers at once and studied the little cardboard guide carefully before choosing as she used to do when she was a girl. I was reminded of her and Waldemar. They had always looked together at the little pink and green and gold pictures of the chocolate wrappings, the circle of delicate invitation. Waldemar, unable to read, made a great study of the coloured pictures of chocolates and never made a mistake.

When Louise offered me the box in the morning I could not accept, regretting my memory, unable to control it. I was about to go up the top staircase to see once and for all what was there when Tante Rosa appeared on the landing, as if from the shadows between the doors, and said to me that Leopold would be grateful if I would go in.

'He wishes very much,' she said in a low voice, 'for you to go in to him. His student is playing for the first time his own cadenza. He wishes your opinion.' So I bowed a little waist bow to Tante Rosa and obeyed.

At last the morning came to an end and Madge and Norman arrived in the old car. Going away for the weekend was for us both a new experience. But no one in the house had suggested we should not go and we left with them all smiling fondly on us.

'We do nothing here but eat,' Madge said later. 'Really it's too terrible but what else can one do in the country?' She looked at me as if to suggest another meaning, but I could not look at her. I sat opposite Louise shelling peas, our fingers working clumsily with the fresh green pods, pod snapping, snap pod. Madge, at the sink, cleaned the fish her husband caught. The fire burned up. The stove was bright and hot and, in the little oven, a duck, stuffed with oranges and cloves, was roasting. A tremendous meal was in preparation.

Norman came and went, his woollen jersey was beaded with drops of moisture. He came into the warm fragrance bringing more fish and more wood. And Madge prepared dishes and mixed things in little bowls and, at last, took everything off the table and spread a cloth and set out knives and forks and glasses. Louise and I were both awkward in our strangeness. I thought Louise was going to cry when she knocked a glass off the edge of the table. Madge consoled. She drew us all together and we became simply people getting ready to eat. Outside, the path of the moon on the cold water was left to shine, shivering, unthought of and forgotten.

Louise's cheeks were very red.

'It is only the fire,' she said when I put my hand on her hot forehead. She ate very little from the piled up plate Madge put in front of her. Norman and Madge ate with enjoyment and I loved Madge for her eating. She offered the remains of the duck and took more for herself with her own knife and fork. We were an uneasy little group staring into the red hot cave of the stove. Sometimes a piece of wood fell and sent up a shower of sparks.

'That's pretty,' Norman said every time. I tried to think of when I had been at the hut alone with Madge but could only remember my own inadequacies.

'Oh you're so beautiful!' Madge had said. 'And your hands, they're so beautiful too but too cold. You can't make love when your hands are so cold.' I remembered only her shudder and her saying 'The only thing I can feel is the coldness of your hands!' I wanted to weep when I thought of it.

I had nothing at all to say to Norman so we sat in silence, Louise taking, with her accustomed gentleness, the affectionate caresses which Madge frequently bestowed upon her.

'What lies at the bottom of the ocean and shivers?' Norman asked us a riddle.

'What lies at the bottom of the ocean and shivers?' Madge repeated, pondering, questioning herself and us in turn.

'I give up,' she said. We watched the game played between

husband and wife.

'You give up?' Norman said, his face short sightedly close to Madge. I knew Madge did not love him and, for a moment, I was sorry for his wasted generosity of love.

'Yes, yes I give up,' Madge said.

'A Nervous Wreck,' Norman's lined, sagging face creased up into a smile which bulged his cheeks. It was his utmost. His thick lensed spectacles shone in the firelight.

'Aw! Get on with you!' Madge was good humoured in the warmth.

'You've taken a chill,' she said to Louise and I loved her voice. The intimate hoarse voice spoke to Louise but it was as if she spoke to me. 'Louise, Pet, I'm afraid you've caught cold!'

And then it came, the arranging for the night.

'Jacob you have the sleepout, it's only very small, pick which bed you'll have,' Madge said. 'We'll be all Girls Together in here,' she tucked her arm round Louise and indicated the double bed in the room off the kitchen. 'And Norm'll have two chairs by the fire here —'

'Oh I couldn't turn you out of your bed!' Louise said to Norman. She was shivering in spite of the hot fire.

There were two little beds wedged in the small room. 'I can sleep there with Jacob,' Louise said.

'Yes,' I said forcing myself to face Madge in explanation. 'Since a week ago Thursday, Louise and I are married.' I spoke in such a low voice she could hardly hear. 'We can share. It is all quite in order.' I explained, keeping my voice soft.

'Oh!' Madge screeched. 'A Honeymoon Couple!' she was very bright suddenly.

'Norm! D'you hear?' she screeched again. 'A Honeymoon Couple! What have we got left to drink?' Norman searched in the unpainted sideboard, diving behind Louise's hot, flushed face and shivering body.

'That'll do! Madge pounced on the bottle. It was nearly empty. We filled up the tiny kitchen, all standing, and drank to our own self-consciousness. We all took turns to go with the torch to the lavatory. 'Normie doesn't mind being last,' Madge turned back the counterpane for us as we shivered in the cold bedroom.

Secretly, I was glad to be in the big bed. The lean-to room was one of the frailest buildings I had ever seen. I thought the beds in it were completely uninviting. Both looked hard and both were pressed against the damp walls. All night Louise shivered beside me though her body was hot. The cold air from the estuary hung over our pillows as if the room had no walls. All night the wide sweep of water sighed along the narrow shore. I thought I could hear someone weeping. Sometimes I thought it was the wind, and at other times, I seemed to recognize the hoarse voice. A woman, alone in the night, weeping. It was a reassurance, a comfort even, to hear Norman snoring. An unbroken rhythm of undisturbed sleep.

It was quite clear the next day that Louise was ill. Madge collected all the pillows and rugs in the hut to make the bed more comfortable. She busied herself looking after Louise and scarcely spoke to me. She put my breakfast, some of Norman's fish, before me and I ate alone in front of the cold stove.

'I suppose you're thinking I shouldn't have let her walk out in the cold yesterday,' were the only words she said to me.

'Of course I don't think so,' I began to say. I wanted to say I had been glad. 'I hoped you'd be friends,' I said. Madge looked up to the low stained ceiling as if speaking to someone there.

'The story of the week!' she said. 'Friends! Whatever next!' And we did not say anything else but I knew when Madge spoke in that way she was desperately unhappy.

Of course Norman used boiled milk, the only boiled milk there was, when he made us some tea.

'With all the fresh milk standing there! Ugh!' Madge said. Her face was swollen and puffy, I supposed from crying.

88

She looked with exasperation at her husband and she tipped her tea into the sink, while Norman and I drank ours with the milk skin floating in patches and sticking to our lips.

XI

There seemed very little for me to do during Louise's illness, though the whole household was absorbed. Sometimes, in the mornings, I walked in the garden to and fro across the uneven courtyard and down to the leaf-thick wall of hibiscus. When I walked like this in the damp morning, the rustling sound of the mulberry leaves detaching themselves and falling made me look up quickly to see if someone was there. Perhaps Waldemar would come shuffling through the fallen leaves and stand before me. But no one was there, only the leaves falling to gather with those already fallen.

I stood alone remembering snippets of silk, fragments of lace, the tiny gold pin on the narrow black ribbon, the shapes and colours of Madge's clothing. Louise just laughed at me when I told her once to shorten her dresses.

'People must wear what suits them,' she said. And I thought of Madge hardly covered by her clothes and Louise buttoned and tied with tapes into hers.

The lampshade, white fringed, in the darkness inside the window of Louise's room suggested the loneliness I felt. As I looked from the outside it appeared as a symbol of the life confined in the bedroom, the life being kept between the walls of the room because of the illness.

I looked up at the white lampshade every morning and remembered the solitude of illness in childhood. Sullenly I took medicine from a spoon held out to me by my father. I remembered how, wishing for my mother, forgetting that she was dead, I refused to look up at my father. Louise's room was not cold and bare as mine had been and the aunts would hover over her. She would look at them and return their smiling looks. I continued to walk in the garden.

'I suppose you're thinking I shouldn't have let her walk out in the cold yesterday,' Madge's voice was bitter. I wanted to comfort her then. Now I could only think and remember.

Madge washed up the cups and Norman went for a doctor. Madge sat beside Louise and tried to soothe her to sleep. I stood in the cold little kitchen and stared out at the grey water. The estuary, Louise's illness and Madge's unhappiness were disagreeable realities.

At last Madge came out and pulled the door almost shut.

'She's sleeping,' she said in her hoarse voice. 'I'm sorry for what I said just now,' she said, and it was like her whisper at the rehearsal.

'Oh Madge!' I said and we held each other close. She was warm. Her fragrance and soft warmth comforted and disturbed me.

'I've been so wretched Jackyboy,' Madge said and her breath caught in a hoarse sob. 'Why didn't you tell me before.'

'Don't cry,' I whispered. 'Don't be sad,' and I kissed her again and again, little soft kisses. My marriage had been a shock to her. How could I ever explain it to her. I could not explain to myself.

She drew away and peered round Louise's door; all was

still. Her dressing-gown fell open and I felt her body closer to me than it ever was before. I could not stop myself. I lifted her to my heart and she seemed to fly to me. I drew her into the lean-to bedroom, my arms around her to guide her on to the narrow, hard, little bed. In my arms she moaned. We rose and fell together in a fierce rhythm and then she called my name.

'Jackyboy!' she groaned and held me harder. I flew and dived and we sank together laughing and kissing.

'That's a very rare thing Jacky,' Madge laughed in her hoarse voice. She seemed to be brimming with tears. We went on laughing.

'Thank you oh thank you,' I said, 'did you know, Madge, you are very beautiful.' I kissed her eyes.

'Oh Jacob! Next to her I am nothing, only old and ugly!' she burst into tears. 'I know I'm ugly and old,' she said. 'And I want to be friends with your Louise but all I can feel is envy. I want you for myself.'

'I want you too,' I kissed away her tears.

'I want to be in your life and to be there when you are playing to Them . . .'

'I know,' I stroked her hair and her face. 'Remember this was very special for us both,' I reminded. We laughed again holding each other.

We had to think of Louise and, of course, the doctor coming. We dressed quickly. Madge was comforted and relaxed. She sang and lit the stove. As the flames rushed up, the firewood spat fireworks in the hearth, it seemed as if the little kitchen was brought back to life.

I looked in, round the door, at Louise. I wished Norman would be a year bringing the doctor and, at the same time, I wanted him there at once for Louise.

I caressed Madge while we waited. Lovingly I pinched the lobe of her ear and put little gentle kisses over her lips and her nose and her eyes, I loved her, quietly close, feeling desire returning.

'Like that, the way it happened then for us,' Madge said

in her low voice. 'It's very rare, it hardly ever happens to anyone like that.' And then she was sad.

'I don't want to give you up Jacky,' she said in such a low voice I hardly heard her, 'I never had anyone I really loved,' she said. 'You are very much loved,' she said, 'everyone cherishes you.' I nodded sadly. 'When I was a girl,' Madge said, 'I wrote a letter to myself from a made up mother. My mother never wrote. I sent myself this lovely letter so that the girls would see the things my mother promised me. She hadn't anything for me really and she never wrote and later I never saw her —' I moved closer to Madge and folded her in my arms.

'Dearest, don't cry,' I said to her and, while I kissed her, I listened anxiously for any sound from Louise.

Walking to and fro in the cold mornings I wanted to tell someone that Louise's illness was tedious. The household was hushed from the moment we returned, a solemn little procession, helping Louise back to Tante Rosa and Aunt Heloise. I longed for Louise to be well, I did not enjoy the house as it was.

'Louise doesn't seem like a real person at all,' Madge said, while we waited for the doctor.

'How do you mean?'

But she did not seem able to explain. She said it was strange too that the only time we had really made love, that was how she said it, was when Louise was asleep just the other side of the half open door.

'We had to wait to have it away together after you were married too!' she said and her laughing was really crying. I stopped her vulgar, sad mouth with a kiss.

And walking through these cold, mulberry mornings I thought about and remembered again and again, in between worrying over Louise, the wonderful moment made timeless by Madge

93

calling out my name so that I knew I could lose myself as I found her.

'Thank you oh thank you,' I said softly and was face to face with the gnarled trunk of the sad mulberry tree.

All the time I talked to Madge, I told her things. Sometimes I talked to Madge while I was playing the cello. During Louise's illness I was practising the cello passages from the Boccerini Cello concerto in G, in particular the second movement. Leopold beating time, not knowing that, with my eyes closed, while I was playing the cello I was talking to Madge.

'Madge I must tell you, when I was a boy we had blue and white crockery. We had feathery plates of willow, bamboo and bridge patterned and the aching domes of my childhood were vaulted in brown linoleum and weatherboard and when the crumpled leaves of the vines were drying and turning yellow they were like shaking profiles of little well bred faces, silhouettes in the damp evening, nodding and shaking towards one another and away as if whispering, shaking again and sighing tiny fragments of messages which could never be communicated in the tremulous movement. If only you knew the leaves of the vines!'

Cello phrases allegro. 'Madge I must tell you how I watched the leaves for hours. When I was a boy Madge I peered into the vine leaves as if I could go through them into some unknown magic place and find out, in the end, what it was they were trying to say to each other . . .'

Leopold stopped my cello and said to go back some bars and he sang the violin and beat time and nodded and I began again to play. 'Madge I must tell you, always blue and white unwashed willow plates and cups piled at the open window and an intrusion of vine leaves jostling. I watched my father as he bent his back over the basin. My Uncle Otto was coming and Aunt Mitzi, fragrant in her furs was coming too. She always smelled so nice, something from the Palace of Perfume in Cairo, she once showed me the little bottle etched with pictures and an inscription from the

94

Tomb of Pharoah in gold on the tiny black label. Something you would like very much, Madge. You would like my Aunt Mitzi, Madge, she is so warm and very kind . . . '

'Play again — adagio,' Leopold's soft voice, so I played, curtained thickly from the rest of the house.

Cello. 'Madge, I must tell you Aunt Mitzi loved the land. "Ah! I love this land," she always said it and she stood looking across the vineyards and my uncle shaded his eyes with his hands as he too looked into the distance which was ours. "Not for sale!" my father said and we went inside to eat the chickens stuffed with mushrooms and chestnuts which Aunt Mitzi had brought with her. While I sucked the bones and licked my greasy fingers she squeezed my arms and legs and felt again my ribs with pink, plump hands.

' "Jacob needs to eat?" she said to my father.

' "He needs to go to school," my Uncle Otto said and, though my father agreed with them for peace, it was some time before he took their advice.'

In the tenderness of the playing of the cello it was as if I spoke to Madge and made love to her. I was exhausted and trembling.

'That is enough for today,' Leopold said and took my cello.

No one reproached me for Louise being ill. She lay ill for some time and I walked alone thinking about Madge and longing to see her. I spoke to her in my thoughts as if I lay pressed against her breasts. My longing for the delight and comfort of her body was more than I could bear.

'Love me, Jacky!' I pretended to hear the hoarse whisper. I put off the loving. 'But Madge, first I must tell you things — "Oh this land!" Mitzi sighed and shook the cloth at the back door. Do you know Madge, she nearly twisted her ankle on the broken step trying to see as far as possible in all directions.

'The land, Madge, it was nothing much with the vines Mitzi said. But for building. A building project. Riverside Blocks. Aunt Mitzi had to adjust her underclothes to accommodate the excitement at the prospect of such a sale. She wore thick lensed spectacles and her eyes shone; they nearly burst through the thick glass. She collected up her dishes, Madge, Madge, I can't love when I have things to tell you. What a talker I am! She, Aunt Mitzi always complained that we never had any clean plates so she brought her own.

'And now the unlimited money I have, Madge. Now after the death of my father I have as much money as I could possibly want.

'I want to tell you, Madge, about Uncle Otto coming to the house.

'"Mitzie had an apoplexy," he explained to us that's what he said. "It was the sale, it was too much for her, in a few days she will be all right," Uncle said. I want to tell you, Madge, I tried to go with my uncle to see my father's vineyards once more. I couldn't go. Madge, your breasts are sweet but I must tell you, my face twisted up. You must have seen my face. I was afraid to go out into the outside world with him. Madge, I was afraid. My face hurt.'

I longed for the comfort of her voice and I thought how she would say it, I pretended to hear the hoarse whisper.

'Never mind Jacky it doesn't matter,' and I thought of her hands stroking my smooth back and her pleasure in the smoothness of my skin. I thought of the desire growing between us.

'I want to see you Madge more than anyone else in the world.' I was standing in the dry, sad leaves under the twisted branches of the mulberry tree. I was quite alone.

Waldemar could have dropped from the tree at that moment.

'Which hend you hev?' His breath smelled of hard boiled eggs. And his two white fists hung before me, which for my choosing, which hend? 'Which hend?' Waldemar's face was bursting with the squeaky laughter wheezing up from the small organs in his chest.

Waldemar's heart was too small, They told me. His heart was too small for the size of his body.

'Oh I'm not playing that,' I said.

'Aw go on! Which hend you hev?' He pushed the white balls of fist up and down, I tapped the left one. Waldemar farted with excitement. From between the fat, white fingers a cockroach fell kicking into the front of my shirt.

When I stood there in the leaves alone under the empty mulberry tree there was no Waldemar, no Louise and no Madge. No one was there.

In the evening I played my cello, alone, for Leopold had to lie down to rest his legs. While I played, adagio, I kissed Madge in my mind, in my thoughts and in my heart.

As the slow days passed I longed more and more to be with Madge. Longing for her became the most important part of my life. I planned meetings which never took place and lived with the joy of meeting and the sadness of parting, all in my imagination. All the time I was on the edge of the household where Louise was gradually regaining strength wrapped in the devotion of her two aunts.

'When you are well,' I said softly to Louise as I sat beside her narrow white bed. She was in her old room protected by Tante Rosa's apartment through which one had to go, as if taking part in a military operation, after leaving the gloomy landing.

'When you are well you must go out into the world, out from this house and see things. Study something perhaps,' I said. 'Have an interesting work somewhere,' I urged in low tones so that Aunt Heloise, resting under her pink eiderdown, should not hear. With my restless fingers I pleated the soft, cool sheet. Louise looked at me.

"Why ever?" she asked and gave a little laugh. 'People should do as they like to do,' she said.

I wanted time for Madge and it seemed to me that this was the only way I could have the time.

'You would like,' I said nodding wisely at her.

'Maybe,' and she turned her face away. After sitting a short time I got up quietly and bent over to kiss her. She seemed to be asleep. Before I left, I opened the window and let the cold air into the room, another idea had occurred to me, something to give me freedom to be with Madge. But the thought was killed at once because, as I left the room, Tante Rosa, the Grenadier in a subdued march, came in and I heard the window being quietly closed straight away.

XII

I bought a little dog for Louise. I went with Madge after a concert rehearsal. She had seen an advertisement. We had to go to an unknown house where I paid a high price for the ugly, little dog. Madge nursed her in the bus.

'I'd call her Daisy,' she said. She looked so happy with the terrible little creature. I wished the dog was for her.

'I'll buy one for you too,' I said. We liked to be on a bus together. It was a time of being alone and I always wished the journey need not end.

Louise took the little dog with a kind of serious pleasure. She stood in the kitchen chopping up celery and vegetable peelings to mix in the dog's food. The aunts too took a serious part in the care of the Fräulein Daisy as she became part of the household. I saw the ugly dog as a way for me to have little snatches of freedom, either while they were all absorbed in the elaborate, careful, food preparations or during the times when Louise would ask me to take Fräulein for her little walk.

Longing for Madge, just for the sight of her, for just a few minutes alone with her, made the house more of a prison. My life began to be a series of contrivances to see Madge. My passion growing daily in my mind became more wildly uncontrollable. I forced myself to be as ordinary as possible in the quiet household. I began to go out more and no one tried to stop me.

Madge and I began to meet. Several times we went to look at houses. Places to rent. We tried the windows and lavatory chains, we opened strange wardrobes smelling the ghosts of clothes and moth balls. In dusky kitchens we came upon strange moulds and forgotten spices trailing from neglected shelves.

A place to be alone together. Sometimes despair crept in with the potted ferns and the table runners of plush. Frilled home-made curtains, holding dust, hanging on rings where a door should have been, we stood alone with the house key in a shaft of dusty sunlight in one of the ugliest rooms I had ever seen, Madge was in my arms at last. She cried.

'It's all so hideous and depressing,' she cried. Half naked in the chill bedroom, no love came from the blurred wall paper, dismal roses in a faded trellis of stripes. The bed rejected.

'Oh how cold your hands are Jacob!' she shuddered. 'Whatever could I be doing here all alone on the days when you couldn't come. And what about the nights? What'll I do alone of a night?'

'I'll come often you'll see,' I tried to comfort. 'I'll buy you an ugly little Daisy dog,' I promised her. Shivering we dressed in the squalid memory. Though Madge made tea and tried to sing in the hostile kitchen our hopefulness ebbed as we set aside the dying tea cups.

'I suppose I should have washed them first,' Madge offered. 'I don't fancy the cups at all.' I shrugged, we wanted to leave the place.

Though I paid in advance for houses Madge never went to stay in any of them and neither did I.

'Never mind,' I tried to comfort her. 'It's just that we haven't found the right one yet. Couldn't we go to the hut again?' I asked. But she shook her head.

'He's sold it.'

'Why has he done that?'

'He had to. His business is not too good and he had some expenses. He misses it.'

'Does he like music?'

'No, not at all. Really not, he's mad on fishing. That's what the hut meant to him. He could hardly bear to sell it.'

'I have plenty of money,' I said, 'I could have bought.'

'No,' Madge said. 'It wouldn't have worked.'

'My money can make all the difference in the world,' I said. Madge shook her head.

'Sometimes you're such a child Jacky,' she said. 'It makes me realise I'm twice your age.' I put my finger on her lips. We were looking over another impossible house.

'Don't,' I said. 'If you could know the difference my money has made to them in that house.' I said. I seemed to hear the girls' voices singing and Leopold, his pure tenor, in the fragrance of freshly made coffee,

> *And every secret sin arraign*
> *Till nothing unavenged remain.*

I sang the two lines.

'What's that?' Madge asked.

'Oh just some Mozart,' and then I said, 'till I came to that house to be a boarder they never had real coffee, Louise told me years ago. There was a great deal they didn't have before I came there.'

'It's quite clear to me they think you are a good investment,' Madge said in her hoarse voice and, in spite of the ugly place, I felt I wanted to love her at once.

'Let me love you,' I took her in my arms.

'Oh Jackyboy I couldn't, not here,' Madge looked about,

her eyes disappearing in their puffy beds. 'We'd feel worse than ever,' she said. 'Let's go, I hate this place.'

'You must always remember that they always loved me and did their utmost for me,' I tried to explain to Madge as we went along the path to the gate.

'Oh yes,' Madge said, 'doing the best for themselves,' she yawned and walked ahead of me filling the narrow path.

In the evening I practised my cello alone, the deep notes sinking deeper, more thoughtful, more tender. Bach, Haydn, Boccarini. I thought of Madge.

The music troubled me. I wanted Madge again. I played badly thinking she might be down there out in the dark street, sadly under one of the little dancing doll pepper trees, hoping for me to come out to her.

I thought she might be waiting out there and I stopped playing and tried again, discordant, unsustained, unsatisfied. I thought of Madge unhappy in the manure coloured sitting-room with Him. Norman, I supposed, would be going over his dockets and account books or rewrapping his products for his display case. I hated Norman. His stupidity disgusted me. I disliked the idea of his closeness to Madge. When I thought about it it would have been easier if Madge were dead. Dead she could not belong to Norman any more. Or, so I thought.

'I think I have just the place you are looking for,' the house agent said to me when I had taken him into my confidence about my requirements. At least as much of my confidence as was permissible in the circumstances. The human predicament cannot be simplified by allowing oneself to be a burden on some other person. Sometimes I longed to approach someone, a stranger, and unburden myself completely. I longed to throw myself upon the tolerance and kindness of this stranger and ask him to listen to all that weighed so heavily upon me.

Of course Tante Rosa, Aunt Heloise, my father-in-law and Louise were always kind and tolerant. They looked upon me with love all the time. There were moments when I nearly spoke to them about Madge and how things were between us. So nearly did I speak of my private, secret life that sometimes I had to leave the room and rush upstairs to prevent myself from telling them.

'Play your cello for us,' my father-in-law, gaunt now with the pain in his legs, said sometimes on those occasions of return after I had been forced to rush from the quiet, half-lit room. We all sat spaced in the cold shadows with distances of floor boards and threadbare rugs creeping slowly between us as the evening went on.

'Play Prince of a Fellow!' He waved his long, white hand to and fro gently beating time. Louise was well enough to sit up, we spent the evenings with the music and Aunt Heloise poured madeira wine and handed us the little milk sugar biscuits so beloved by Waldemar all those years before.

Louise went to bed early, Aunt Heloise followed with a shawl. I went with Fräulein round the dark streets hoping I would find Madge waiting, patient with love, under the next tree.

I made an appointment to go with the house agent to see the place and, later, met him and we went there together.

At once I was agreeably surprised and pleased for the house was set far back from the road in extensive grounds, secluded, thickly shrouded in dark trees, imported pines. I liked them. The house itself was protected by a battlement of balconies and verandahs. The garden was overgrown, leaf-green walls of oleander and hibiscus, left to themselves, had become impenetrable. The whole was surrounded by a high brick wall and the wrought iron gates could be locked from the inside. I noted the agreeable fact that the neighbouring houses were sufficiently far away to ensure the necessary privacy.

To please the agent I praised the comfortable armchairs and the mirrors in the hall, and I agreed with him that the extra closet with lavatory and wash-hand basin were an essential.

'These are the only doors on the ground floor,' the agent told me; he showed me the patent device for locking and double locking the front door, he assured me that the windows had special locks and that there were double storm doors at the back of the house.

'All the doors have chains,' he said, supposing in a well-bred way, hinting, that I had very valuable possessions.

'Well most people would not think so,' I said looking aside, turning my twitch into a laugh. 'There is always the odd crank who covets what the rest of the world would not think valuable or even sane to possess,' I said. I wished I had some strange possession, an ornament or a picture or even a manuscript which might be considered valuable enough to be stolen. How could I explain that it was something about my life, something strange, peculiar to me which must be accommodated.

'The house belongs to an opthalmic surgeon and will be vacant for one year, possibly longer,' the agent explained to me in his quiet voice. I thought about the houses for which, so full of hope, I had paid six months' or even a year's rent in advance only to find it impossible to start living in those places though they seemed as near to what we needed as possible.

'Sing something,' I said to Madge in the kitchen of the last house. Madge tried to clear her throat and sing for me in the hoarse subdued voice I loved so much but the hopelessness of the sad way we were living made her voice crack and she could not sing. This house would be different I could see at once. It was spacious and comfortable and had an atmosphere about it, something of the well-being of wealth. I had been stupid to look at the other houses and to try to install Madge in any one of them. Here she would feel at home and why not, I had the unlimited money to provide everything of the best for her.

I followed Mr Williams through the kitchen, the sculleries and the outhouses. He was proud of the pantries and the still-room, not many houses now had them. None of this fitted in with my problem but I tried to pay attention and look pleased. He was so anxious to please me.

The waiting-room and the consulting room on the ground floor would not interest me, he thought, but I asked to see them. I was enchanted with the consulting room. It was the black velvet curtains; the room was hung on all sides from the ceiling to floor with them, the windows, behind the curtains were shuttered. I could not hide my pleasure.

'I had never thought of black velvet curtains,' I said to him.

'But what about the apparatus, the chair and all those heavy books, you wouldn't want them and what about these?' he indicated the glass case of instruments, the enormous leather topped desk and swivel chair, all of which took up a lot of room.

All this would not interfere with what we wanted.

For a moment I gave myself up to the idea of patients huddled in the other room waiting to crawl helplessly, eyes full of pus or overgrown with fungus; afflicted by the pain and soreness of eye disease indicative to the knowledgeable surgeon of soreness and disease in another more intimate part of the body, into this magnificent place where hope and salvation awaited then in a quiet, dignified atmosphere.

There was a grey carpet on the floor. It was fitted into all the corners, it was soft and deep and thick. I thought, with pleasure, how it would be possible to be in this room without anyone in the rest of the house being aware of it. The door was lined with baize and, with satisfaction, I saw there was a sturdy, brass bolt. I tried the bolt, it was effortless and noiseless.

I was engrossed for a time in sliding the bolt to and fro, lock the door, unlock the door, lock the door and so on.

Possibilities went through my busy mind and it seemed that They could all, Tante Rosa, Aunt Heloise, my father-in-law, the sewing machine, Fräulein, my wife, our music, everything could be accommodated on the upper floor. And above that the attic rooms would be Waldemar's and down here I could be with Madge. What a house! for a year or longer. Oh the possibilities. My heart leapt at the ideas as they came.

'There is a housekeeper and a maid should you require them.' Mr Williams interrupted my reverie with the bolt and we started off up the stairs. I felt uneasy straight away.

'Their rooms are at the top of the house,' he said.

'Are they here now?' I asked. I was anxious suddenly and felt disinclined to see the rest of the house.

I tried to recapture some of the rapture of the velvet curtains but thought instead of these women, the housekeeper and the maid lurking somewhere about the house, watching and listening and whispering together while pretending to be engaged in their work, the housekeeper and the maid sitting in their discreet sitting-room too concerned over what should concern me only.

'They are on holiday in the country,' Mr Williams was saying. 'But they can return at a moment's notice, their references are excellent. I have copies of them should you wish to see them.'

'Later, later, perhaps.'

Mr Williams suggested we start at the top so we went first to the rooms set aside for domestics and the nurseries. Rooms reminiscent of the warmth and safety of childhood without a hint of the shuddering, muttering, mocking nightmare which belongs with childhood. There was still a rocking horse and a dolls' house and a scarred table and all the usual furniture battered and now discarded.

Waldemar would have more room.

'It is an old family home,' Mr Williams said with pride. We went through the lavender and jasmine guest rooms, through the bathrooms, newly decorated in pink and black, and white and gold, then into the master bedroom and the second and third, everywhere agreeable, very clean and comfortable.

'Shall you want so many rooms?' Mr Williams asked me gently. I was suddenly terrified of my own face grimacing, leering, twitching, a tunnel of faces in the mirrors. I plunged ahead of Mr Williams trying to control my face, avoiding the mirrors, assuring him that I needed a large house, throwing the words back over my heaped up shoulder.

I looked quickly at him to see if he had noticed anything strange about me. He was pulling aside heavy, rose-pearled curtains for me to look out into the secretive depths of the dark trees. He wanted me, he said, to enjoy the colours of the furnishings while there was still daylight.

In the dining-room he opened sideboards and the canteen, and waited for my glance of approval at the elegant cutlery and at the glasses and the silver.

'I'll take the house,' I said. 'For one year, possibly longer.'

We went down together. Mr Williams was quietly pleased. I found him a most agreeable companion and, while I wrote my cheque for a year's rent in advance, I thought I would ask him to have dinner with me. I had come to like being with him. Perhaps we could talk together. I had an overwhelming wish to spend the evening with him talking to him. He told me I could have copies of the agreement and he said he hoped I would enjoy living in the house, but I broke into his well-bred little phrases.

'Would you care to have dinner with me this evening?' I said trying to sound casual, careless even, about a little dinner.

'Well thanks ever so much I'd like to,' Mr Williams said.

'What about seven o'clock then, at the Adelphi? Don't be late!'

And then I remembered the servants.

Scrambling somewhere, struggling, crawling from a sunbaked furzepit, bedraggled and unwashed; they must return from their holiday in the country and hasten to put on their clean, freshly ironed uniforms to come into my service. The housekeeper, hunting out her keys and her white caps, and the housemaid begging a pin, for she has been neglectful of buttons.

I was thinking what to do.

'Oh the servants?' I said.

'When would you like them to return?'

I took a fresh cheque and making rapid calculations, I wrote quickly.

'Here are the wages and a living allowance for them both, for the year,' I said. 'Please be so good as to convey it to them together with my regrets and whatever other messages you think appropriate.'

Mr Williams glanced at the cheque and muttered something about my fabulous generosity and we parted, for the time being at least.

I wanted to meet Mr Williams again. I wanted to talk to him. I wanted the relief of his company and his attention and his understanding and I wanted his sympathy.

At last it seemed that I was going to be able to talk over with someone the details of my voluptuous and horrible unhappiness. I should feel the same kind of relief as a secretly crippled man would feel if allowed to roll off his stockings and reveal his deformity to a surgeon accustomed, every day, to seeing the bent and the twisted.

Though I wanted to meet Mr Williams again I knew that I was not able to do this, even though it was all prepared and arranged.

Not half an hour after we parted, I went to the Adelphi and left a message, faintly scented and embossed in gold, for Mr Williams. I wrote that I was detained and that I hoped he would dine, in any case, at my expense. And I thanked him for everything.

On the way home I stopped at the florist and selected damp fleshy stalks till I had an armful of heavy headed flowers. I sent the girl from the florist across to the station for chocolates and then I went home to Louise.

'All the world loves a lover!' Aunt Heloise opened the door and drew me into the large room where they sat shrouded in the long, drawn-out evening. They took the flowers and the chocolates and exclaimed with pleasure.

'A very Good Evening to a Prince of a Fellow!' my father-in-law called out. He was on the chaise-longue with both legs raised as blood poisoning had developed from the varicose ulcer. He clapped his long fingered hands in welcome.

The little table was there, lace covered, and arranged with sweet cakes and the milk biscuits, madeira encased in frail wickerwork and, this time, crême de menthe for the aunts.

Louise sat beside her aunts, her hair soft on her sweet neck. She had on her brown dress with the crocheted collar. It was my favourite dress. It was now I should bend over her and murmur my love to her with a kiss but I thought instead of Madge and wondered whether she was in bed already safely asleep.

'How is the Great World outside, my Prince of a Fellow?' my father-in-law called. He had the draughts set out beside him, he always had the black ones. He was waiting for a game.

'How is Tante Rosa?' I asked, 'And Aunt Heloise?'

'Say something nice about Tante Rosa's hair,' Louise whispered. 'Aunt Heloise was two hours arranging it.'

I said something nice and Louise told me softly how they all were and how they had spent the day, what they had said and what they had eaten, and slowly I began to die with my dying thoughts there in that room till I did not even reach out in my thoughts to Madge any longer.

'So Prince of a Fellow! I challenge you to a game!' My father-in-law was waiting so I played draughts. Aunt Heloise poured the wine and offered the sterile biscuits.

'Take Fräulein for her walk,' Louise said to me in her quiet voice later. 'And will you please observe her bowels. If necessary walk around twice with her.'

'I followed Fräulein's squat spotted body as she waddled along the pavement. We had the night, fragrant with jasmine, to ourselves and I stepped into my dream of Madge and I thought about the house. It was mine for the year and it was there for Madge if she would go. It was there for all of us if I could move everyone. As I walked I thought out elaborate ways by which we could all be there, all of

109

us so that I could be with Madge and with Louise without the embarrassment of knowledge and explanation.

XIII

I could think of nothing else but this house. Mr Williams delivered a package containing the keys, Tante Rosa kept it safely in her room and gave it to me without questioning.

The next day I took Madge there and we searched the house for unwanted occupants, servants or thieves or the owner unexpectedly returned but no one was there.

'Don't be uneasy,' I said to Madge and I took her into the consulting room and closed the baize covered door.

'See the little bolt,' I said and, laughing together, we bolted the door and unbolted and bolted. I kissed her and unbuttoned her cheap blouse.

The extraordinary feeling of privacy in the room was wonderful. We looked at the desk and the leather armchair. Madge spun herself round in it, her hoarse laugh was so funny. We chased each other round the cabinet of opthalmic instruments and caught each other in front of the bookshelves.

111

The severe titles quietened us, we stood in front of them like two reprimanded children.

'Oh think of this carpet!' Madge whispered. 'What it must have cost!' And then she said, 'Where's the kitchen again?' We went back to the kitchen and Madge peered into the tins and jars and then we went out, the householders, to do our shopping. We chose black sheets and an orange counterpane, and in a supermarket, we chose pickles and a chocolate cake mix and marmalade and soup and I patted Madge and stroked her when no one was near. Once I pinched her nipple through her blouse and she screeched in a hoarse whisper and upset the pyramids of cereal. We left then, laughing, secretive, alone together, pleased to be in among the other people who knew nothing at all about us. We took back the shopping. It was as if we were encapsulated, as if living on an island of our own.

'If only it could last for ever, this being together,' Madge sighed. 'I think I'll have a bath,' she said. I went up with her and watched her.

'You go down and get us something to eat,' she smiled lazily from the hot water. So I obeyed. In the kitchen I looked carefully for an intruder but all was safely locked up.

'I heard about the chocolate cake so I thought I'd come along,' and there Madge stood, covered in scented foam, dripping in the doorway. My laughter bellowed among the basins and saucepans and lost itself in the armchairs in the hall. I took her polished bubble covered body in my arms, my desire was the only thing that mattered and we went, almost without time, to the consulting room.

'Bolt that door!' Madge began to peel off my clothes. I pulled her down on the thick carpet covering her with my kisses.

'The floor's the best place,' Madge said softly.

'Jackyboy!' she called, it seemed as if the whole room and the desk and swivel chair turned over and over.

'The floor *is* the best place!' Madge pushed me aside singing in her hoarse voice, she leaned over me caressing me with her big soft breasts. The grey carpet held us as if we were floating.

'I want it again.'

'Don't be greedy!'

'Please!'

'It's the best part, afterwards, when you call me your Darling,' Madge said.

'It's because of what's gone before,' I said.

We went naked to the kitchen.

'That cake will be a biscuit!' Madge said. 'And why the hell we bought sheets and things when we don't even need the bed!' She laughed till tears ran down her face.

The kettle had boiled dry so Madge heated water in a saucepan. We sat feeding each other with sliced ham and bits of crystallised ginger. We poured wine generously, filling glasses for each other.

'Will you stay here Madge,' I asked her.

'All alone?' she asked.

'Well you could hardly bring Norman,' I said.

'Will you be here?'

'Not all the time, Madge, you know I can't.'

'I'd get the creeps at night,' she said. 'Jacky I love you and would do anything in the world for you,' she said. 'I want to be wherever you want me, you know this, but I don't think I could stay here alone all night. Can't you stay? Please stay Jacky. Just this once.'

A great sadness engulfed us. I knew I couldn't stay away from them. I began again to think of my plan.

'We'd better get dressed Dearest,' I kissed her. 'I'll take you home. We can come back again. It's mine for a year.'

I was thinking how I could bring them all to the house so that I could be with Madge. They could come there as a kind of holiday, a house on the river, what could be better. I'd tell them it was to be a holiday, they need never know Madge was in the consulting room and she need never meet them.

113

'Would you stay if there were other people, tenants, upstairs and you just were here in the consulting room with the little washroom and your own little side door in and out of the house?' I asked. 'And me near you?'

'Well it wouldn't be so creepy with noise and people above,' she said. 'I'd have to tell Norman something or other though. What will I tell Norman Jacky? I'll have to tell him something. He is my husband after all. What'll I tell him Jacky?'

'Later, later,' I brushed Norman aside. The evening was filled, clouded really by more than Norman. An uneasiness came into the house as if they were there already changing the secret luxuriousness into the economical cleanliness in which they lived.

I thought of Waldemar wrecking the upper floor. I would have to think of some way of letting them move from that house to this place so that they could bring Waldemar without my knowing anything about it. I dismissed thoughts about the mess he would make, the house was mine for the year after all. I had paid and the owner, the opthalmic surgeon, a rich man, must take his chance. I unlocked the kitchen window and threw the burnt kettle and the bits of uneaten food in to the darkness.

'One more time?' I asked Madge. She was poking the velvet curtains in the consulting room as if feeling for an intruder. She shuddered and peered behind the end of the curtain.

'Enough's enough,' she said and kissed me and I felt the reassuring perfumed warmth that always came from her.

'What will you do about Him?" I asked in the hall.

'Oh Norman,' she said. 'I'll tell him I'm leaving him,' she said lightly. 'I'll tell him I can't stand the way he sits down and squeaks his chair. I'll tell him I hate the way he eats and sleeps, I'll tell him I hate him,' she began to laugh in a way I couldn't understand and I wished for her hoarse voice. I went into the little washroom and left the door open.

'Hey Niagara!' she shrieked, ' where streams of living water flow, ' she sang, 'Old man River! All ober de hallway! Poor teddy's tiddles,' she said, 'we've been overworking him. Talk

114

about water works!' the hoarse whisper of her laugh comforted me.

I thought of Norman alone in the little brick house sitting in one of the round, blue armchairs, his feet in carpet slippers planted side by side on the manure carpet. I thought of him like this, sad and perplexed because of Madge leaving. He did not deserve to have someone like Madge I told myself. If she left him it was his own fault. I felt he must smell like manure somehow in that stuffy little house. Because I did not care about him I wasted no time being sorry for him.

Exhaused with the day, too tired even to mind leaving Madge at the corner of her street, I stood in a yellow pool of lamplight and watched her disappear. Leaves rustled along the pavement, chased by the restless wind. White moonflowers, hanging in clusters over the boards of a fence, gave off a sweet scent. The white flowers shook and nodded. Melancholy of the most profound sort settled on me. I walked slowly by the dark houses and, leaving the fragrance of the warm restless night, I went indoors.

The large room was filled with music. A new record on a new gramophone. Mine. Boccarini, cello concerto. From his chaise-longue Leopold was conducting an invisible orchestra. Tante Rosa, Aunt Heloise and Louise formed an audience of devotion. Devotion to the music and to each other. I paused in the folds of the curtains of the door, the cello bringing tenderness up from my heart.

My hands smelled slightly of my time with Madge. I tried to keep the secret scent in my nostrils, trying not to breathe in the heavy fumes from the kerosene heater which was always, even on a warm night, in the alcove of the great window.

I wanted my life with Madge and I wanted my share of this love and devotion and the perfection of the music. I waited and watched while Leopold brought the final movement to the conclusion. From his chair he bowed to his small audience. Louise took off and put away the record and Aunt Heloise brought the sweet biscuits and the wine.

115

I had eaten too much already. I pushed the plate aside.

'Ho there! Prince of a Fellow!' my father-in-law tapped the draughts board but, in my lethargy, I sank into a chair. No one asked where I had been for so long.

'But my back. My shoulders!' I said to Louise in a petulant voice.

'Rosa! Heloise!' Leopold called his sisters. 'The Prince is exhausted tonight, he must go to bed!' Louise helped me out of my jacket and shirt and rubbed my shoulders with camphorated oil so that I was soothed and comfortable. The sadness I felt after I had been with Madge slipped away as Louise cared for me.

I could not sleep and, with all the wine I had been drinking that day with Madge, I was thirsty. I went down in the night to fetch some water.

I found Aunt Heloise sitting alone in the cold, empty kitchen. She had a decanter and a wine glass in front of her and a piece of stale pastry in her hand.

''It is my name day, my birthday,' she explained. 'I am drinking port wine and thinking of all my other birthdays all the years ago.' A smile appeared on her kind old face. 'Wine?' she offered.

'No, I want water,' I said. I fetched some for myself and drank it off like a sick man.

'It must have been sixty years ago,' she detained me. 'When I was only nine years old, imagine! a clergyman friend of the family, families had friends in those days, you know the sort of thing, an extra place laid for dinner and people for a game of cards in the evenings; well this friend, the clergyman, gave me a pair of fancy garters.' She laughed to herself. 'Rosa too, she had a pair, bright green. Can you imagine, Rosa! Mine were rose coloured with rosettes of black lace. They don't make that sort of thing any more.' She refilled her glass with the beautiful red wine and stared at it. She still had the cake in her hand.

'We never wore them, Rosa said we should keep them for best. But I ask you when does one wear best garters?'

And she crumpled in a broken kind of laugh.

'Happy birthday, Aunt Heloise,' and I bent to kiss her soft face. She drew me to her ancient mauve dressing-gown; the scent of old age enveloped me.

'I hope you have not bought anything too expensive,' she murmured as I stood empty handed before her. 'Sit down,' she said and I drew up one of the scrubbed wooden chairs.

'I have been thinking and thinking of the mountains,' she said. 'You will not know about mountains. I missed the mountains when we came here all the years ago,' she said. 'Mountains, mountains and mountains and the snow, thick snow or a fine powder of snow and the clear air and then, in the spring, the snow melting and the rushing of the water from the melted snow. But never mind. I must not bore a young companion. Wine?' she offered, I shook my head and she poured again for herself.

'Eat your cake, Aunt Heloise,' I reminded her.

'No, you have it, young people like cakes. You have it for my birthday.' She sipped from her little glass. Her creased cheeks were flushed.

'Don't give me an expensive gift I do not expect it,' she said and then, as if recollecting, she went on, 'So many houses in the war were requisitioned, you know, one had no choice, families were crowded or split up. Some never saw their children again. Strange people inhabited the privacy of one's house. In our house were officers, fine men in uniforms, very well mannered always *Gnädige Fräulein* and a salute but can you imagine the hours they kept and their boots!'

'Come to bed, Aunt Heloise,' I said in a low voice.

'You know,' she made her voice even lower than mine, 'though we were alone I always felt it was not quite all right —' she paused and in a lower voice she said, 'but in Vienna, in the war, we became suddenly poor, desperately poor, we seemed to lose everything,' she said, 'so what could we do?'

I patted her plump shoulder. I supposed the port wine had caused this confusion and confessing. My head ached

117

but I felt I could not leave her alone on her birthday. A mouse ran across one of the scrubbed tables. From the dark corners of the kitchen came creakings and rustlings.

'It doesn't matter,' I said gently to her.

'Shall I come up to bed with you?' Aunt Heloise looked at me tenderly. I shrank from her with exhaustion and embarrassment.

I drank two more cups of cold water and then helped myself to some wine. I sat down again on the other scrubbed chair.

'Happy birthday to you!' I sang. We touched glasses, smiling. The kitchen was so clean, what could a mouse find there? I thought of Louise spending all her life scrubbing the tables and chairs. I thought of her lying alone in the big white bed.

'I want to tell you about a house, Aunt Heloise,' I said. 'I want to take you all for a holiday; it is a beautiful house. The garden goes down to the river where there is a little sandy beach where no one would be except ourselves.'

Aunt Heloise listened while I described the rooms and the elegant furnishing, the good quality cutlery and the fine glass and china.

'Oh very nice, dear Jacob,' she said. 'Oh, very nice house.' She did not believe in the house or think I was serious.

'You know,' she said suddenly, 'Rosa too, you know, not just me. Can you imagine, Rosa?' She began to laugh and I saw the tremulous movement of her wrinkled old breasts, but there were tears in her pale eyes. 'Can you imagine, Rosa? I wanted to see for myself — when Rosa, you know, to see what it was like with her, she never spoke about it, Rosa always so silent. I climbed up, you know, there were fanlights over our doors. Such a beautiful old house. I climbed. I put a chair on a table and dragged it to the locked door and I climbed up to see, but I was not nearly tall enough,' she sighed. 'My thighs are very short you know.'

'Aunt Heloise, I want to tell you about the house,' I said firmly. 'I want us all to go and stay in this lovely house, it is on the river. It is to be a holiday for us all.' I took her hand and leaned over to her telling her seriously, 'this house, Aunt Heloise, looks from the back, right down and across the river. How the sun sparkles on the water! And right outside the big windows is a fine garden with lemon trees and little steps cut in the cliff and, just now, the whole place is covered in bright yellow flowers, such a cheerful colour! It is to be a holiday for us all. I can do this.'

Aunt Heloise listened to me. She patted my hand with her free one.

'I have plenty of money, you know this don't you,' I said.

'But what about Waldemar?' Something fell softly in the corner. We both glanced across but nothing moved.

'So he is up there then?' We looked at each other.

'Yes, Jacob. He is there all these years.'

'So I did not kill him that day.'

'That is right.'

'Why is this? How could you do this?' The haunting fears came crowding back and the remembrance of uncertainty. Of course I had half known all the time but the half knowledge only served to make the truth more shocking.

'Waldemar did not ask to be born,' Aunt Heloise whispered in tenderness. 'Leopold could not bear to put him in an Institution. He knew so well, or thought he knew so well the conditions of such a thing. He tried. He tried but he could not. He could not bear for Waldemar to be taken away without some kind of explanation to help him to understand. You know Jacob, one couldn't explain anything to Waldemar. And you know, Leopold couldn't bear for Waldemar not to have the things he loved and he, Leopold, was afraid they would tie Waldemar into a bed with bars.'

We were silent for a few moments. And then Aunt Heloise said; 'What is a man in any case, a little bit of meat and a little bit of bone and he only walks about for such a short time. Who knows if what a man does is good or bad? And who can know really why he does what he does?'

We sat with the quiet half-dark kitchen all round us. It

was as if we were in the middle of a strange sea, as if none of the familiar things were near.

'Leopold had no choice as Waldemar grew older,' Aunt Heloise explained. 'He knew he could not keep Waldemar, and then the answer came when you came. For us, you saved Leopold. He was able to keep Waldemar where we could watch over him and love and cherish him. Waldemar was able to hear our voices and to see us and we could be with him. Perhaps you will try to understand.'

'But I had to be — Murderer.'

'No, no,' Aunt Heloise whispered. 'Don't shout!' her soft knees pressed against mine. 'You were a Prince, not a Murderer. You killed no one. You were given all our love and care and you have all the freedom. Do we ever ask where you go or what you do or what you think? We teach you, it is true, all these years and look after you but as a Prince not as a prisoner. You will never understand enough Leopold's love for you. We all love you so dearly, Jacob,' her eyes filled with tears.

'But Tante Rosa hates me,' I said putting my hands over my face.

'No, Jacob, never! It was fear you saw, fear only. Rosa feared for your well-being, if you did not eat well or sleep well. She fears that we do not repay our debt to you well enough. Rosa is her own severe wardress. A keeper of herself.'

'You owe me nothing,' I said.

'Of course I don't mean the money.'

'I understand that.'

'We have all loved you so much,' she wept again and I tried to console her.

'We have hard times,' she said. 'You wouldn't understand; all — all the large houses were taken. I cannot describe what it is like to have one's home taken away and used by uninvited people and then we were not used to poverty. But, as you see, we learned to work and make for ourselves a new life and get for Leopold the books and things he loves and needs. Rosa, you know, was very clever, she smuggled things out to Switzerland. Quite early she was very clever.

'I was so homesick when I was first here. I hung up our cups on zese hooks and with every cup I put on the hook I said to myself the name of a loved one and I sang to myself the tune, *die Forelle,* you know, Schubert, *The Trout,* and then my tears came and after this my heart was better, not so heavy you understand. Always, Jacob you know, when you get up in the morning think of someone you love and think everything well for the ones you love and think you will like the work you must do. And then you will like.' Aunt Heloise sighed, 'But sometimes I have been so tired and I have had to sew all night with my legs aching so. Sometimes when I help Leopold to be comfortable on his chaise-longue I have wanted to cry out "let me lie down too, my legs hurt, I too have enlarged and painful veins."' She sat grieving over the past. She was talking about the war and their flight from their own country. I knew they talked of those times when they sat together during the long quiet evenings.

'Your coming meant a great deal to the household,' she went on more clearly. 'It is not easy with one's needs and refinements to adapt to a new country. It was all so strange, language, customs, climate everything. I always thought Rosa was too hard on her. She, Rosa, insisted that Leopold send her away.'

'Her?'

'Yes she was a Jewess, she couldn't make the changes. Because of her we had to flee for our lives. Leopold tried to help her, her mind was frail and, even with our love and help and Rosa's stern help, it was not enough.'

'You mean Waldemar's mother?'

'Yes, she is also mother of Louise of course.' Aunt Heloise paused and went on, 'Of course when you came, and your uncle paying so well for you, things changed very much for us and we wanted with all our hearts to help you.' She pushed the piece of cake towards me. 'Eat Jacob, you must be hungry now.'

'So you let me think I had killed Waldemar!'

'No. No, not that. You must not think in that way. Not like that.'

I thought about the money from my father's land. I thought how he had toiled in the vineyards and suffered from hardship and how he had worked, all night sometimes, in the little shed, making casks and I thought how easily I had become rich because of the place where his land was and the need other people had for it. And I thought too of Louise and how she loved me. I thought of my marriage, and again felt this sense of isolation as if the familiar scene of the kitchen hid something unknown and frightening. Aunt Heloise spoke again with the privileged intimacy of old women.

'We love you, Jacob. It is something special to be loved and one should be grateful for being loved and it is a privilege to love. There is so much in the word love. Leopold, especially, loves you. He wants you to be the finest cello player in the world. A Prince of the Cello.' She began to weep softly again.

I put my hand across to her.

'Don't cry, Aunt Heloise,' I said to her. 'Don't cry, think instead about the holiday I have planned in the beautiful big house I have taken for all of us.'

'But what about the baby?' Aunt Heloise looked up.

'What baby?' I felt angry with Aunt Heloise for making herself so stupid with too much port.

'Louise's baby, of course,' she said.

I sat back from her, amazed. Louise had never said anything about a baby. The knowledge that Louise's baby was not mine, how could it be, was like an intolerable pain. A physical pain, somewhere inside, which made me feel sick. I tried, at once, not to think of the night when Louise had pressed herself against my useless body. As on that night my mouth now seemed full of the freshly laundered pillowslip. I stood up, scraping the chair back on the floor. I looked down on the bedraggled mauve dressing-gown; Aunt Heloise looked like a heap of discarded clothes. I felt a deep pity for her and an even deeper one for Louise. I shivered as I forced myself to think of the embrace wherein her child had been conceived. Most of all I felt sorry for myself. I wanted to cry and rage and to strike someone. Still looking down at Aunt Heloise I said as quietly as I could, 'Yes, yes, of course. Of course, the baby. Well, we might go after that.'

I helped Aunt Heloise up off her chair and I helped her to climb the stairs. With surprising speed and silence she slid from my arms into the dark gulf which was Tante Rosa's room, passing on into the blackness beyond, where her own bed waited for her.

For reasons which were inexplicable I stood on the landing an hour later and played my cello. At the foot of the flight of unvarnished stairs I played without care, with discord and noise. Ugly cello. Either I did not disturb anyone or they chose not to reveal that they were disturbed.

XIV

'How's Teddys tiddles today?' Madge was already at the house. When she opened the front door she looked as if she lived there. The sight of her dressed in an apron delighted me.

'Guess what,' she said, 'of all things, he wanted to come with me today. "I'll take a day off" he said to me this morning. Imagine! You can guess how I felt. "Well at least we'll have lunch," he said. The cheek of it! "Norm," I said, "Norm, you'd better get lost," I said to him. "I've a couple of appointments to keep," I told him. "N.O." I said. "N.O. No. I can't break 'em." I said before he could get in one more word. I've had a job to get rid of him I can tell you. Anyway, thank God he's gone off to work. Really business is that bad, he can't afford to slack off. It all depends on what he does himself how he gets on but let's forget him. Come and see what I've been doing.' She dragged me into the consulting room. There were flowers everywhere and a coloured rug on the plinth.

'Did you remember the salami?' she said, 'you're very late. I thought you were never coming. Where have you been?' She kissed me and pressed herself against me. There was something exciting and yet safe about being close to her. I longed for that forgetfulness which her wonderful body could give.

'I want you now. Come on!' she urged me. Her voice made me wince. 'Hurry! Hurry!' she said.

'Madge,' I said, 'there's something I have to tell you.'

'Later,' she said, kissing me, 'it'll do later. Love-love you so Jackyboy!' I had to hold her off with both arms.

'Madge,' I said, 'I have to tell you that Louise is having a baby.'

'Good on yer! My very word! The story of the week!' Madge turned her eyes up to the ceiling so that they became puffy slits with only the white showing. She drew breath sharply and gave a kind of subdued shrieking moan, long drawn out, through her clenched teeth.

'Don't Madge! Please don't!'

'You're a fine one for surprises. You really are!' her changed voice had that lightness I disliked. It was her way of showing unhappiness. She sat down in the swivel chair, small and fat beside the great desk and the cabinet. She started to turn in the chair. She turned faster so that, when it was spinning fast, her laughter, shrieking and wild, seemed to come from everywhere.

'Don't Madge! Don't! Please **don't** Madge!'

Slowly the chair stopped spinning. It was at its greatest height.

'I guess I'll have to go back to Normie,' she slid dizzily from the chair. 'At least he don't hurt me the way you do with your family's dirty washing.'

'They're not my family they're . . .'

'Well, what are they then. They're feeding off you aren't they. You're so intelligent,' Madge's voice rose to a scream. 'You're so intelligent and yet you can't see people for what they are. Blood suckers!' she spat.

'Now just a minute Madge. Madge. Dearest let me . . .'

'Oh! and I'm not any better. How could I sink so low. Oh Jackyboy. What am I saying. What am I saying. What has happened to me!' She howled aloud.

'Madge! Madge stop, please.'

'We can't go on like we have been,' she sobbed.

'Why Madge. Why not Madge. I love you,' I tried to put my arms round her.

'Because an icicle melts that's why,' she said. 'Oh Jacky what's the use. What's the good. It can't lead to anything. I want you and you want me. You can't be in two places at once. No one can be two people.' She took off her apron and folded it.

'Oh don't take off your apron. I like it.'

She shrugged. 'When's the baby due anyhow?'

'Now I suppose. I mean, soon. I'm not sure. Madge you must believe me but I knew nothing about this baby. It's been a shock to me.' I wanted to her to comfort me. 'Madge, I swear the baby is not mine. I love you. Please believe me.'

'It doesn't matter to me whose it is, really, as if I care what you've been doing or not doing,' her voice rose again into that lightness of insincerity. 'What does it matter,' she said, 'all that matters is that she is going to have a baby. Go home and look after her. How can we go on with all this?' She waved her short, thick arm in the direction of the rest of the house. 'What's the point of all this really?' Her eyes were again brimming amber like cat's eyes ready to spill golden tears. She crouched down with her face in her hands and cried quietly.

All the things she said I knew were true. I wondered how I could have allowed myself to be married to Louise. I reflected on the way in which everything had taken place, in a sense, with my consent and, at the same time without it.

While I was with Madge all that other life, Louise, the cello, Leopold and the Aunts seemed unreal as if I had read about it in a book. Yet when I returned to the house and to them it was as if I had never been away. Lately my old fear had come back and I had started to prowl about again trying to discover some trace of Waldemar. In my mind was the monstrous embrace which had given Louise a child.

'Oh! how often!' I heard the little moan escape from my own lips as the uncontrollable thoughts went through my mind. I wanted to know whether the love-making which had given her a child had also given her desire and satisfaction. As I watched Madge kneeling on the carpet sobbing I thought of Louise and her straight young body and I thought of her small, exquisitely white breasts.

'Oh! how often,' I moaned to myself. 'How often did they and when.'

Madge cried for some time. I tried to comfort her. Later she was quiet and she telephoned the warehouse to leave a message for Norman asking him to come home for his lunch.

'I think it's better that way,' she said. Her face was swollen with crying. The sight of her made my heart ache.

'I think I ought to tell you straight away,' she said, 'that I don't really like music at all. You know, it doesn't really mean a thing to me, specially the cello. I only play the violin because I have the skill. It's just a job, just play for the money, that's all.' She was busily renewing her face from various little containers she had in her handbag. I sat, exhausted, in the consulting room chair watching her.

'As for that music teacher of yours,' she pursed her lips for the frosted colour, 'that Heimbach, who does he think he is? And what's a tin pot small town orchestra? I mean, what does it mean to play either a violin or a cello in that orchestra. What kind of standard do we have? What great standard does that phoney Heimbach have? They're having you on. You play well Jacky but there's playing and playing. Take it from me, that lot have latched on to you and they've got you where they need you.' She snapped her handbag closed and stood up straightening her clothes, 'I'm not just saying things out of spite,' she said, 'I just think you ought to take a close look at what's going on around you, that's all.'

I had to agree the baby looked like me. They all said so in low voices nodding round and round the wicker cradle. The baby's hair was thick and dark like mine. There was something wonderful and perplexing about this new little creature, a baby girl who had waited to be born, who had come, with nothing whatever to do with me, to be my child and Louise's. The household was full of preparations, shawls and baby clothes and mysterious packages. And there was too the voice of the baby. She seemed to cry in a heartbroken way as if with some inner knowledge of the grief of the world into which she had been brought. It seemed to me that her crying was a sadness.

Every day I stood beside the dainty cradle watching the little head turning and pushing uneasily towards the rolled up piece of sheet Aunt Heloise had tucked down as protection from the woven cane.

'Her hair is dark like mine,' I was quite prepared to take on my new position. After all Madge had said it did not matter whose baby it was. She was there in the cradle. She had to belong to someone. Tenderness for the little round head and the small helpless hands welled up in my heart. I stroked the baby's head with one timid finger.

'All babies have dark hair to start with, she will be blonde later on,' Tante Rosa said, her lips hardly moving. Her grim face frightened me. I wished Louise would whisper one of her little explanations.

'It is only one of Tante Rosa's headaches.' But just now she was bent over the table, with her back to me, folding layers of white material, carefully folding and smoothing as if this was all that had ever to be done in a person's life. Her conspiracy with the piles of cloth on the table made her seem far away from me as if I were seeing her in a dream and not able to reach her. Perhaps the experience of childbirth took a woman to remote places beyond understanding. I thought I could wait for Louise to return. This thought faded quickly as did the new pose I had taken up. The dark hair would change to fair and the thickness to a kind of wispiness. Without meaning to continue to think in this way I knew that they all knew things which I did not know.

Without wanting to, I began to think of Waldemar. The day I punched him he had eaten hard boiled eggs, one in each hand, one after the other. His breath, wheezing, smelled of them. I thought I smelled hard boiled eggs and turned to see if Waldemar had come. It was only Aunt Heloise standing and nodding and smiling, agreeing with Tante Rosa that babies, of course, never kept their first hair. My lips twitched and my whole face seemed possessed by a painful muscle. I was smiling and my dry lips were caught, cracking back, over my teeth so that I could not stop the hideous grin. As I left the room my distorted face grinned at me from the tarnished panels of the samovar, long unused on the dresser. In the doorway, half hidden by the thick curtains, I paused in my crooked flight and looked back. Louise gathered up her baby, tucking the soft shawl all round. She sat down and unbuttoned her dress and put the baby to her breast. Tante Rosa was on one side of her and Aunt Heloise on the other, their heads bent together over the intimate whiteness.

Le bonheur du ménage, I remembered the title of a painting. Why couldn't I be part of this *bonheur*. Nothing was mine. I ran from the folds of the curtain and, as the door closed softly on my heels, a sob burst from my heart. I ran along the passage to my old room and wept there as if I were still a little boy unable to bear the separation from my father and the vineyard as it had once been.

Louise's confinement was something like her illness. The whole household was occupied with Louise and her baby. Though now, at the time of the birth, the mulberry tree, at the end of the garden, was in full, thick leaf and covered in berries. The air every day was warm and heavy with the over-ripe fruit fermenting.

I spent a great deal of the time with my father-in-law. I played the cello for him. We played draughts. He always had the board set up beside his chaise-longue. We had soup and a particular kind of cake brought to us at intervals on a tray by Aunt Heloise.

'It is like the old times,' Leopold said, eating his cake with pleasure. 'This cake, Jacob, was always made in the old times, once a month for the washing women. A special cake made only for the washing women,' he held up his piece of cake and looked at it with delight. 'And now,' he said, 'I am able to have some every day!' Aunt Heloise took the trays away and sponged the soup stains from Leopold's waistcoat.

My loneliness was unendurable and sometimes I went out from the absorbed household. I had to make excuses and tell lies to Leopold. Tante Rosa and Aunt Heloise worked endlessly from a very early time in the morning until the evening when they could sit in the big room and nod and murmur to each other. This sitting time was shortened by their leaving to go with freshly washed and aired baby clothes to sit with Louise while she fed the baby.

Every night I stood outside the house in the dark street holding the end of a leather lead while the squat, ugly Fräulein Daisy nosed about in the leaves. She had become a quiet little dog and seemed to have no wishes of her own. I regarded her as a stranger and a nuisance. When she was pleased about something and wagged her grotesque body as she tried to wag her tail I felt awkwardly sorry that I had no real feelings for her.

I supposed the little dog was lonely like me. I longed to see Madge. I wanted her. Every hour of the day I thought about her. I tried to play the cello but could not. From his chaise-longue Leopold shrugged.

'Put the bad cello to bed,' he said, dismissing it with a wave of his white hand. 'Improvise,' he said and pointed to the piano. I sat down.

'What shall I play?' I asked him.

'Ach!' he said. 'He asks what he shall play! Improvise! Prince. Compose. Now is the time to compose, *weil ich niemals dich anhielt, halt ich dich fest,* take the poem. Compose where I left off, *because I never held you, I hold you forever.*

'Finish the Rilke song for me.' He sang:

> *'Look, when the lovers start*
> *confiding the thoughts of their heart,*
> *how soon they're deceiving.'*

I played the piano badly. In my heart I talked to Madge with all the tender words I could think of. The night scented trees over the warm pavements and the futile little walks with Daisy made me want Madge. I forced myself to stay away from her. I waited about near the cradle and smiled at Louise, watching her from the outside of the guarding circle of Aunts. Louise and I were never alone together. She seemed withdrawn and she kept her eyes from looking into mine. This was because of her unfaithfulness I told myself and yet, I knew it was because of mine. I had no doubts about Louise's passion and, in my more honest moments of reflection, I knew that I was not capable of rousing or satisfying it. Neither of us spoke of Madge or of the visit to the hut. It seemed to me now that Louise must have seen and known everything, even though ill and apparently asleep. I felt sure now that I had seen tears overflowing slowly from beneath her closed eyelids.

I walked alone on the waste land encircling the swamp. Pale, dead trees stood there. They seemed to rise higher out of the water as the evening advanced. The croaking, sighing and rattling of frogs filled the stillness. I wondered, when I walked, who could live there so near all the rubbish which was brought there every day. I wished that I was safely inside one of the ugly little houses with Madge. Sometimes when I walked there at night, I looked with longing at the lighted windows of the houses. The whole swamp was ringed with smouldering fires, flames leaping up here and there as if an unseen power was in attendance. There were uneven beaten tracks, short cuts to different kinds of rubbish. There was a sharp smell of rot and decay. At all times of the day and the night a faceless tractor jerked and bumped to and fro pushing and grinding bottles and tins, old clothes and unwanted furniture, into the sour ground. The swamp water oozed up steadily, spreading slowly like melted butter.

I walked alone beneath the high walls of the hospital where I had gone, as a boy, with Leopold, and on to the cemetery. On the other side of low hibiscus hedges the graves were clean and flat like neatly made beds, all facing in the same direction. I thought of the bodies being comforted in the earth, returned to the earth, buried deep in clay. Sometimes I longed for the real and the last burial.

'Land for sale. Six foot of land cheap.' I thought I was dreaming. 'Still a few blocks left, pick your choice!' the hoarse voice changed into a smothered laugh and there on the other side of the flowering hedge was Madge. Face to face across the trembling leaves, I did not even wonder why she had come to this remote corner of the cemetery. She parted the bushes and pushed her way through; it was as if we were quite alone in a world far away from the squat brick and concrete suburb.

'It's pretty ragged here,' she said, her eyes, just slits, were full of merriment. She had on a pink dress and stockings to match. She sat down heavily and stuck her short, fat legs out. She looked at them.

'Colour of pig!' she grunted and panted and scuffled about on the dry grass. I sat down beside her and kissed her again and again.

'Oh why do I love you so much,' I heard her little moan. 'Oh go on! Don't stop now.' Then she pushed me away. 'No Jackyboy!' she laughed 'we can't do it here. Not here with all the dead people around.'

'They're all asleep,' I said kissing her again.

'God! I'm starving!' Madge stood up.

'I think we left food in the house didn't we?'

'Come and Get it!' Madge shouted.

Madge was so impatient to unlock the front door, she split a fingernail.

'Curse!' she sucked her finger. 'Hells Bruddy Bells.' Quickly we went all over the house to make sure no one was there. The whole house was serene, clean and quietly waiting.

'I love you when you sing,' Madge said, 'what is the song?'

'Oh was I singing?' Madge and the happiness of being with her in the house filled me with music. The comfortable proportions of the walls and the windows and the glowing colours of the furnishings all blended into a sense of well being. Desire was in all the armchairs, every picture in the house seemed to depict desire and passion.

'Sing, I love you when you sing,' Madge said in a whisper. So I sang:

> *'Come to me, I'm coming to you,*
> *you must answer me, my angel ...'*

'Oh, I love that!'

'It's Brahms, a folk song.'

We lay together, naked, on the soft thick carpet in the consulting room.

'You are beautiful.'

'So are you.'

'Sing some more.'

'I can't, it reminds me of . . . Oh! I can't go on like this,' I cried to her and it was all over before we had really started. Madge kissed and comforted me. We tried again to love but noticed, instead, all sorts of stupid things like the dust on the ledges; Madge wept and I began seriously to console her, stronger and stronger. Full length, my body stroking her body, and she responded. Slowly seriously, more seriously, stronger. Stronger.

Somewhere outside dogs barked insanely. I was anxious about the dogs. Madge moaned and strained and clasped me with her thick legs. Pink, pink legs. The consulting room

133

disappeared in our laughter.

'Dustbin men! Dogs always bark at them,' she rolled over and sat up.

'God I'm starving! That was pretty good, eh Jacky?' We went together to the kitchen.

'We can't go on not being together,' I told her. I stroked her shoulders and her breasts. 'It's not fair,' I said. 'I want to get them all to come to this house and you can be here too.' I said.

'You'll never get them to agree,' Madge said.

'I'm going to have a try Dearest,' I said to her. 'You see I really can't live without you.'

I did not dare to be away too long. I left Madge, cursing her broken nail, at the end of her street. I hurried back, the perfume of the afternoon hovering faintly about me, stronger in the palms of my hands as I lifted them, cupped, to my face.

'Soup for the Prince of a Fellow!' my father-in-law clapped his soft white hands. My supper was brought in on a tray. The draughts board stood ready at my elbow. Aunt Heloise sat opposite Tante Rosa. They were playing scrabble. Louise sat beside them watching.

She smiled slightly as if enjoying herself. The aunts talked in low voices, their eyes watching closely the pattern of the words. Their voices, however, suggested another subject.

'Neppmädchen! Goldgräberin,' Aunt Heloise said, 'how do they call such a one. Gold Digger!' she said.

I thought, at first, that they were talking about their game, or that they were making a joke about the baby or perhaps, in a playful way, teasing Louise. But they were not smiling and, in the tone of the conversation, there was nothing amusing.

'Sie ist eine die auf sein Geld abgesehen hat,' Tante Rosa spoke with the soft s of the Viennese pronunciation. Her lips hardly moved. 'She is after his money,' she hissed. It was as if she held herself still in a pain she could not speak of.

Because I was thinking of Madge, it seemed to me that they were talking in this way of her. I dipped my bread in my soup.

'Do you like your soup?' Louise would have whispered to me once. 'Do you like it? It is a five bean soup, see the different beans, a special recipe from Tante Rosa. Tell her that you like her five bean soup.'

I wished for Louise to whisper to me but she appeared to be absorbed in the game her aunts were playing. She scarcely seemed to notice I was there. I tried to make her look at me and dropped my spoon. At one time she would have fetched me another.

What gold could Madge be trying to get? How could she be looking after or getting hold of money?

As I sat there, crumbling bread into the soup, I thought that there must be some way of telling them about the house on the river. I tried to think of a suitable way to suggest my plan to them.

Aunt Heloise, who it was said had been playing badly, looked with complacent affection on the word she had made.

'I have no letters left!' she said, 'therefore I am winning!'

's.e.l.b.s.t.m.ö.r.d.e.r.' Aunt Heloise spelled her word aloud. *'Selbst* was already here,' she said, 'I simply add *mörder.'* She looked at Leopold. 'Help me,' she said, 'against this cruel judge. Tell her my word and how it means.'

'Self. Yes.' Louise said, 'but self murder, what is that?'

'Perhaps,' Aunt Heloise said, 'perhaps *Freitod* is a more modern word, but I have not the necessary letters.' She looked at Louise. 'In this game one makes what one can out of what one has, *nicht wahr?* Is that not so Rosa?' her voice was strangely hard and satisfied. Tante Rosa nodded her narrow head, a tiny smile appeared in the corners of her mouth.

'Freidtod?' Louise said.

'Have you forgotten all your German?' Leopold smiled at her. 'Literally,' he said, 'free death,' he paused, 'suicide', he said.

'It is,' said Aunt Heloise, 'like a bee, jumping, diving into the honey. He sees the honey and walks into it.'

'But the bee doesn't want to die,' said Louise.

'No,' Tante Rosa joined in. 'No, but the bee wants the honey. She dies because of trying to get what she wants.' They all laughed softly together and I watched them through the steam of my soup.

Louise fetched the baby. She sat down and unfastened her dress and began to feed her.

'Le bonheur du ménage,' I said. My voice, as in a dream, did not carry across to them.

'She will lose her mind when she gets old. And he will become a melancholy old man,' Tante Rosa continued the previous conversation in the same monotonous tone. 'Of course, she has not one word to say for herself. She is, how shall one say, she is nothing. Furthermore, it would be expected that she eats tomato sauce with everything.'

I thought they must be talking about Madge. Madge was in my mind all the time. I thought they must know whenever I had been out, where I had been, they would know everything about me, and they would know everything about her. In my turn, as before, I would prowl and discover for myself about Louise and, though the thought filled me with disgust, about her lover.

'Now! What about our game Prince of a Fellow!' I moved over and took my place by the chaise-longue. Leopold and I stared for some time at the draughts as they stood in innocent readiness to be moved by forces outside themselves from one place to another on the board and off the board.

XV

Days went by, one day after another. Every day was like the day before. The baby was cared for and meals appeared at their usual times. Instead of playing the cello I went round the house looking into one room and then another. I paused in the square of sunlight on the landing below the top stairs and then went on into the rooms, one after another, as though with some purpose in my mind. Something had happened to the little Daisy dog. I was not required to take her for her walk. She had disappeared. Since she was not mentioned, I did not ask about her. At night sometimes, I thought about her pink body and the way in which the pinkness showed through her white hairy coat. I remembered too the busy pleasure she had in nosing through dry leaves along the dark pavements.

There was a purpose in my restless movements, I hoped to come upon one of them alone in a room, in a place, where I could, with a little confidence suggest the holiday in the house on the river. It seemed impossible to break into the baby's routine. There was never a time when I could bring in this extra thing, the idea which I was nursing in my mind.

Whenever I could not see Louise I imagined her up in that hidden away place at the top of the house. The plain staircase seemed neglected and unwatched. There were times when I could have gone, unobserved, up to the attic rooms. Every time there was a chance I did not take it.

The Friday concerts came and went as a part of the regularity. Madge whispered behind the flaps of music in her old way. Sometimes I caught fragments of her conversation. We did not speak to each other, being careful to maintain an apparent lack of interest.

My loneliness had assumed monstrous proportions. I had neither one thing nor the other. At the concerts it was painful to see Madge and hear her and not to be able to go off with her to some private place. At home in the devotion of the household I had no place. I would have liked to kiss Louise in that special spot, the delicate nape of her neck, as she bent over the cradle. I wanted to be in the little, safe circle of love with Tante Rosa and Aunt Heloise as they waited for the baby, Elise, to fall asleep.

Aunt Heloise was playing the piano and I listened to the music. I felt I could overflow with tenderness. Louise was kind and she had loved me once. I wanted, as I listened to Heloise playing, to tell Louise that I loved her. I wanted to remind her of things we had sung together.

> *What shall my guilty conscience plead?*
> *And who for me will intercede*
> *When even saints forgiveness need?*

Heloise was playing Mozart. I wanted to make up my mind to give up Madge for ever and to somehow get out of the mess I was in and to save Louise from what I thought she was doing.

The piano playing soothed.

'Requiem,' Leopold said, 'is like a lullaby. *Kind im Einschlummern,'* his voice trembled. Elise had been crying and the household all took part in the joy felt at her falling asleep.

'A *Wiegenlied,'* Leopold said, he opened his mouth to sing. Instead of the cradle song a long moan came from him. Suddenly his face was changed, he was very pale and bluish shadows spread across his nose and chin. For some time he had had more pain in his legs. Both legs were heavy and swollen and he never moved from the chaise-longue.

'Ach! oh weh!' Heloise was at his side to support him.

'Tante Rosa!' my voice hung echoing in the hall. 'Tante Rosa! come back quickly!' I waited to hear her footstep. There was nothing for anyone to do. Leopold's tired and congested heart had stopped. He died in the soft warmth as Heloise rocked him in her fat arms.

'It's because of all I have done for him, I miss him so much.' The long cry at the grave-side burst from Heloise. Tante Rosa had to hold her to prevent her from sinking down with the damp earth into the grave. On the day of the funeral it rained without stopping for several hours.

For some days the sky was grey with cloud. The sudden and, for me, unexpected death of Leopold brought one memory after another, sharply. I realised how much I had forgotten about him during his painful bed-ridden state. I remembered, without wanting to because it was painful, the walks across the waste land to the hospital. I recalled his patient kindness with the sick women and the pleasure his singing classes brought them. He was patient with me too, he had let me take off my shoes and walk barefoot on lawns where sprinklers cooled the grass.

Leopold believed that one lived in order to please others. He was always telling me that my singing would please people and that my cello playing would 'enchant the whole world', as he put it. All his patient teaching, beating time, repeating and repeating. I thought of all the things he had taught me. When I thought of the silent devotion all poured out in my direction, the waiting at the edge of the stage, out of sight, for hours on end, I felt worthless and selfish. I despised myself and, for the first time in my life, wept with real aching grief for the sake of another person and, for the first time in my life, I was not weeping for myself but for him and his life of endless suffering which I had not even begun to try to understand.

I did think, too, that there was now one less person to be considered in that difficult manoeuvre ahead, one person less to be moved to the riverside house.

XVI

During the next few days I tried to assume some sort of control over the huddled women. The baby, Elise, had become fretful.

'Why is she crying all the time?' I demanded, trying to look angry.

'The milk has gone,' Aunt Heloise explained. She looked at me, her crumpled, shapeless face was flushed. 'Louise has lost her milk.'

'Well don't cry about it,' I spoke even more sharply to hide my anxiety. 'I will go and fetch something from the chemist. Never mind! Never mind!' I said to Louise. 'I will fetch something. Don't cry. Crying won't brıng back the milk.' I longed to comfort her.

'Now I must tell you all that I have a surprise for you. We shall all have a little holiday,' I said later on. We were in the kitchen, the mid-day meal was spread on one of the scrubbed tables. There was a pleasant fragrance of cloves from a tray of hot baked apples. Since Leopold's death we had eaten all our meals in the kitchen; perhaps it was to avoid the emptiness of the chaise-longue upstairs.

They raised their sad faces and looked at me. 'I don't mean we shall do something frivolous,' I said quickly. 'I mean, it is to be a rest and a change for every one of us. In a nice, clean house. Louise,' I said, 'you will love this place, in half a minute you can be at the edge of the water. It's very pretty.'

I described the house to them. My voice trembled. It might be too soon to make the suggestion. I was not even sure now that I wanted to include Madge on the edge, as it were, of their lives. I talked rapidly. I felt the enormous house weighing on me. How could I tell them that the river house could accommodate Waldemar. I had no idea whether Heloise had told them of her talk with me. It was possible she did not remember it herself for neither of us ever mentioned her lonely birthday night.

'How is the house yours?' Louise asked me, speaking on behalf of the aunts. 'How is it yours?' they wanted to know.

'I have taken it with rent, you understand, like I pay rent on this house so I have on that beautiful one.' I hurried to explain, 'I pay rent with the idea that we all go. I meant Leopold too, you understand, but of course . . .'

They nodded, they understood. Elise pushed her head and creaked in her cradle. They all understood, more things, than I did. While I told them about the house I realised that I would welcome the chance to stay in the house without the complication of Madge. In my eagerness to convince them my passion drained away.

'Thank you Jacob,' Tante Rosa smiled as far as her severity allowed a smile, 'you are being most kind and generous. I will come with you this afternoon and look at the house.'

Louise looked pleased. Her white, almost transparent, face made me sorry over her. I wished we were close as we had been as children.

142

Aunt Heloise nudged my arm with her plump shoulder, 'Thank you Jacob, perhaps we shall all come soon.'

I left the house at once, having dressed with care. As I began to think about Madge I thought less about Louise. Wanting Madge I bought an expensive car, cream coloured with red leather upholstery. I hired a driver for the car,

'I will provide you with a uniform,' I told him, 'but this afternoon you will come in these clothes. I have not time for everything today.' I asked him to wait at the end of the street where Madge might come, but she did not come.

Tante Rosa sat in the comfortable new car. She did not ask any questions but looked out of the windows. She remarked once that the trees by the river looked inviting. I tried to imagine what it would be like to be taken for a drive with Madge, not having to pay attention to the road, beside me. I could not disregard Rosa's presence. I stopped thinking about Madge.

Tante Rosa liked the house. She walked all round it. She went through the rooms making kind remarks about the furniture. She seemed much smaller. I was surprised that it was a thin, poorly dressed woman at my side speaking with reverence.

'Yes, yes Jacob it is all very nice,' she said.

I thought how easily I could slip from one *bonheur* to the other, from one *ménage* to the other. A little patience, a great deal of money and some arranging and we would all be in the house. The arrangements must be started at once I told myself on the way home.

There was a smell of something antiseptic everywhere. Aunt Heloise, late in the afternoon, was scrubbing and washing the linoleum. Shining wet floors lay beyond every half open door. She, looking tired and, I thought, guilty, was finishing the work as we came in. She seemed to be trying to hide something unpleasant. The sharp smell of the disinfectant must be to hide a dreadful secret. I wondered what could have happened. Heloise disappeared with Rosa; it was time

143

to do something to the baby.

On the landing there was a pile of broken crockery swept neatly into a corner, a fiercely bent fork was on the stairs. I ran along to my room. I wanted to write a letter to Madge to tell her that everything would go as planned. The thought of writing to tell her that we would soon be together was very pleasant. I would contrive to divide myself between the two parts of that remarkable house. Aunt Heloise must have dropped a tray. Perhaps she broke the antiseptic too. There was such a strong smell, it caught in my throat and made me cough.

'Dearest Madge,' I wrote, 'It is all settled. Tante Rosa loved the house as much as she can love anything. I can't wait, Dearest, to have you there all night.'

As I went down to post my letter I saw both the Aunts alone with Elise. They were busy at the table, in the upstairs sitting room, changing her clothes. I stuffed my letter into my pocket and I turned and ran, like a thief, up the top flight of stairs and into the musty passage. I stood still to get my breath. I heard someone snoring. I pushed open the door and saw Waldemar naked, asleep, on a dishevelled bed. His blonde hair was long, it was almost white. With a shock I saw that what I thought was a smooth, dark, silky beard under his full, wet mouth was the long, dark hair of a woman. She lay as if crushed under the weight of the huge body. Her legs, in knee-length, mulberry-coloured, leather boots were crossed over the fat, white buttocks. The long, sharp heels of the boots seemed to pierce his flesh as though, by her act, she had pinned him to her. A mixture of disgust and fear, sadness, horror and pity filled me for it was Louise lying there with Waldemar. Whatever I had imagined, it had not been like this. I turned and stumbled out of the room.

'I should not have come,' I said the words to myself. I asked myself why this should happen to me. I thought I should go back into the room and tell them I was sorry, tell them I was going for a walk, tell them anything.

'Sorry,' I said in the passage as people say it who have

144

intruded. 'Sorry!' I went slowly downstairs.

'I am just taking a short walk under the trees,' I looked in at the aunts. They were still playing with Elise.

'Of course Jacob,' Tante Rosa almost smiled.

'A month on the river will be so nice,' Heloise said, 'Rosa is telling me all about the house Jacob.' Elise lay on the high table between the two old ladies, she was a big baby and was, when she was not crying, docile.

I went out. I thought I must escape and meet Madge. I must see her at once. I hoped she might be waiting for me somewhere on a street corner quite near. She might be there hoping I would come out for some reason.

I ran out into the garden, across the courtyard. I had to run away from them. Straight away I was under the mulberry tree surrounded by the oleander and other overgrown bushes. Where was there to run to? I turned from the wall of leaves and flowers and ran towards the side of the house. I caught my foot and fell headlong. I fell full length, my body on the body of Madge.

She was covered up, rolled up in a piece of carpet. Leaves and earth had been scraped up over her.

'Oh Madge, whatever are you doing here.' I tried to uncover her. She was warm and heavy. I struggled with the edge of the carpet. She was not rolled in very tightly. She seemed to flow out into the leaves and dirt, her clothes all torn, her white throat pricked and stabbed. Her face which was blue and swollen, was not like her face. She was spoiled and dirtied and smeared with blood. Her own blood. She was dead.

The light was fading. I bent close to her calling her by name. I told her I loved her. I begged her to be alive. I put my hand on something hard in the leaf mould. Something sharp pricked into my hand. When I looked, I saw it was the hideous piece of jewellery. It was the grotesque appliance with its food encrusted, crooked wires. Waldemar's false teeth.

The smell of the damp earth and the musty carpet and the sweet smell of blood made me feel sick. In my throat was a painful retching. My head was bursting. I tried to howl with sickness and rage but nothing came out of my mouth.

I ran straight up to the room on the first floor. The two old ladies, their backs arched with devotion over the baby, turned to me.

'We are still talking about the house, Dear Jacob,' Aunt Heloise's old hands were busy rolling Elise into a folded blanket. 'We shall all enjoy the holiday so much . . .' she said.

'There isn't going to be a holiday,' I screamed. 'What filth has been through this house!' I shook Aunt Heloise. My hands sank into her soft body and her head wobbled on her neck. She looked at me her eyes bulging. She was terrified.

'What happened while I was out? What are you hiding?' The baby began to cry. I could not see Aunt Heloise, only Tante Rosa was there, very dark and tall. Her eyebrows gathered into that straight line which crossed the bridge of her nose. It was the face of her headache.

'Be quiet, please, in here Jacob,' she said. 'In this house I give the orders.'

'Grenadier!' I head my own scream. 'Madge is dead out there. How! Why!'

Louise came quietly round the half open door standing half hidden in the folds of the heavy curtain. She was dressed in her usual dress and her hair was neatly plaited and pinned up.

'Ha!' I heard a mad laugh, it came from my own painful twitching mouth. The pain attacked the side of my face and went down my neck, drawing my head down to my shoulder.

'Where are your boots my lovely,' I managed to sneer, 'where are your boots my lovely!' Immediately I was sorry. I did not want to hurt Louise.

'Oh Louise,' I head my own voice sobbing. 'Louise, what is all this! Why!'

Louise simply stood by the curtain in silence. She did not look at me but gazed at her aunts.

'What happened to Madge?' I screamed. 'What was Madge doing here? Why was she here? What did you do to her?'

'Who,' said Tante Rosa stepping forward, 'who is this Madge? what is this Madge?'

I picked up the kerosene stove which was always burning in that big, cold room. I threw it with all my strength across the room. It burst into flames immediately. Tante Rosa was quite hidden in the leaping fire.

Everything reflected the flames. We were surrounded by fire.

'Cover up the mirrors!' I screamed at Louise. My own reflection, twisting and grimacing and distorted, frightened me. The little lace covered tables and the wicker trunks containing our household treasures and money were being eaten by fire.

Through the smoke I saw Louise obediently fumble with the first velvet cover.

'Stop that!' I cried. 'The whole house will burn! Get some water you fools! At once!'

Louise did not appear to hear me and she continued to cover the mirrors as I had told her to.

XVII

'My aunt is lying down. She has a headache,' I heard Louise telling the police. I watched Norman from behind the bannisters. From my place half-way up the stairs I looked down on his white head. I could hardly recognise him as the same man who carried freshly caught fish into the hut. He did not look at all like the Norman whose cheeks swelled with laughing when he told his stupid riddles.

He had to identify Madge. He looked small. He had deep lines in both cheeks as if tears, all night, had made grooves.

Norman did not know what Madge was doing at our house. No one could provide any answer. No one, it seemed, had seen her there.

'Yes, my brother is sick,' I heard Louise explaining. 'Yes, he is upstairs, in the top room. Yes, he stays there always because he is sick.' Her voice was calm and clear. She had to offer explanations.

While the police were there Elise cried and Louise gathered her up in her shawl to soothe her.

Norman looked across at Louise and her baby. There was a sadness in his eyes. I pressed my teeth into the woodwork of the bannister to prevent myself from crying out.

'Can I hold her?' Norman took Elise from Louise. He jogged her in his arms, peering into her face with a tenderness which made me realise how much he must have loved Madge. I felt ashamed.

'My aunt was out. So was Jacob.'

'All afternoon?'

'All afternoon.'

I had to answer questions too. Trembling violently, I called out from the staircase.

'It's all my fault,' my voice was only a whisper. Louise's eyes were like two lamps. Norman looked at me kindly as I came downstairs. Louise kept on looking at me.

'Jacob is very upset,' she said. 'He has hurt his hand on the kerosene heater. We had a little accident with it. See, we have all bandages and my other aunt, the one with the headache, she has bandages too.' She smiled at the police.

'I am afraid my brother is more sick than we thought.' I heard her voice. 'I am afraid he will have to be taken away. We always tried to put it off, but now, well, as you can see ...' I watched her eyes shine as she spoke.

Aunt Heloise sobbed aloud. 'But no!' she cried. 'They cannot take him! Will they look after him properly? There are special things he needs — my poor, poor boy. Ach! oh Weh!'

'Of course, Aunt Heloise, of course.' Louise put her arm round Aunt Heloise.

Waldemar would be sure to howl and fight when he was taken away. He would protest in a heartbreaking way, Aunt Heloise said so, she said that Waldemar loved his home. She said he was the only one who really loved for the sake of loving. She sobbed and prayed by herself. When the ambulance came, I hid in my little bedroom, my old room.

I crouched hidden, but there was no noise at all.

'Up here, please,' I heard Louise's clear voice. I heard the men going up the unvarnished staircase. Then there was the same noise as they came down.

'They gave Waldemar an injection, a sed-a-tive,' I wanted Louise to whisper an explanation. But she explained nothing. We sat in silence at one of the scrubbed tables eating a kind of pudding made from semolina and jam.

The pain in my hand was worse than any pain I had ever known. I cried aloud with the pain when Louise changed the dressing. She never said anything.

'How do you think she feels it.' She could have nodded her head towards the darkened doorway across the landing.

'Go and think of something nice to say to poor Tante Rosa,' I wanted Louise to whisper to me behind the door.

'We all love you, Jacob.' I wanted to hear Aunt Heloise.

'Good evening to a Prince of a Fellow!' I could not bear to look at the chaise-longue and the little cane table where the draughts were set out. The lace table cloth was burned and the table itself blackened.

The pain of the burns and the heartache and the loneliness all seemed intolerable as the days passed slowly.

We all had burned hands from trying to put out the flames as they surrounded Tante Rosa. Because Dr Horowizc was lying at home unable to raise his head or to speak, paralysed from a brain hemorrhage, there was no doctor.

'Louise, we must get another doctor. Can't we ask another doctor?' My voice whined in a disagreeable way. Without proper treatment my hand would be disfigured, destroyed and useless. She, with her mouth full of safety pins, shook her head and bandaged my hand with a clean bandage. Her own hands were bound up in strips of soft rag. There was never a sound from her or from Aunt Heloise when they attended to each other's dressings.

'Everything will be right.' I longed for Louise to say something to me. She hardly spoke. She hurried about the house, cleaning it and looking after her baby. She took turns with Aunt Heloise sitting beside the quiet narrow bed where Tante Rosa lay, burned to death, though we did not realise it at first.

When Madge was buried I did not go to stand beside her grave. Possibly Norman stood there alone. He came to stand with us at the graveside when Tante Rosa's funeral took place. For some reason he came to the house often, perhaps because Madge had died there. He always said he was just passing and had called in because of this. At the funeral I noticed the deep, brown sunburnt creases in his neck. He told me later that his work, being out of doors, made him look as though he was always on holiday.

After the funeral I went down to the kitchen to fetch water to drink. The house was dark and quiet. I thought someone was in the kitchen with Aunt Heloise. Her voice was talking up and down, up and down with the soft Viennese *s* sound siss siss siss. 'Now siss red one, now siss blue one, now siss red one,' her voice talked on. She was standing alone at the scrubbed table; little dishes and ramekins were in a ring on the table, she was adding the small earthenware sauce pots to the plates and cannisters.

'You stand in siss place and you in siss one, you here,' up and down her voice talked to the coloured tins. With her old hands trembling as they hovered over the table, she reached out to move a broken dish. 'Ach! you are broken. You go over there, end you, you are not a broken one, you can go and sit wiss siss broken one. Help him to feel better *nicht wahr*? So you make him better.'

I went out into the hall.

'Louise!' I called. 'Louise!'

My voice reverberated in the hollow house. I heard Louise cross the landing upstairs.

'Louise! Come please come! Heloise and the cannisters are talking to each other. Louise!'

XVIII

Dear Jacob thanking for your letter. As you know I never write letters. It is a great effort for me to write. I am not young as I was also in English is not easy. Your uncle too is not young any more. He is walking in sticks. I myself thanking God have excellent health. Every day I am washing all over with cold water. It is something good for the circulation also I make air baths once every week in different parts of the body. This is good I am telling you before to try but will you listen to me. Never.

You ask me what is happening to your money. You say you never told how much money you had. How could I tell you. Land is only worth what peoples will pay for it and for long times now there is not money about. Every body is always saying all the years you were such a Genius and must not be disturbed and troubled in your music with vulgar things. So you know nothing about the costs of dividing up land and the money which must be paid in fees and in taxes to the government. I suppose that just from appreciation of your Genius I should working all days and all nights without any dollars for my workings?

When I am hearing that they make your money in parcels like refugee I become ill. I am never so ill in my life before. No one has money in packages any more and if the packages were burned in the fire in the house I am thanking God is my money not there too. I am ill whenever I think of money in flames. Also when I think of these people. Always I am trusting only myself. If you are salesman it is a work I know well from when I am a young woman. If I can advise you sell something and before door closes you get order for next week — something else. I walked with a pram to sell. For you with a car should not be too hard.

Mitzi

XIX

Often I asked myself why did Madge visit the house that afternoon.

There was plenty of time for thinking as I went about my lonely existence as a door to door salesman. The hut, the rented house by the river, the consulting room, Tante Rosa's visit to the house because of the idea of the so called holiday, all these things were often in my mind. In spite of going over the events of my life I could find no answers. What was it Madge had wanted that afternoon. Not her death, I was sure that the idea of danger had never occurred to her.

I never spoke to Norman about her. He helped me as much as he could. I never looked into his face directly. He came often so that he seemed to be a part of our little household. For him, every week, Louise put on her best dress.

Norman enjoyed his food, he praised the indifferent meals we had. The Sunday dinners came one after the other. Every week he knocked a quiet knock on our front door at twelve o'clock.

Years went by. Elise was a big girl. She was easy to please. She liked sweet things, honey and sugar biscuits. She was like Waldemar.

Louise withered as the years passed. She cleaned everything thoroughly and went to the factory every day.

In spite of Norman's encouragement I went out less and less. I had no energy for selling. I sat at home waiting for Louise to come, though we scarcely said anything to each other.

One day Louise came home early.

'Why are you home so early, Louise?' Her white, thin face made me anxious. She coughed all the time. Sometimes in the night I was impatient and complained.

'For heavens sake stop coughing! You stop me from sleeping!' When she tried not to cough I lay awake waiting for the next attack.

Louise came home early and undressed and lay down in the cold uncomfortable bed.

'Louise don't go to bed now,' I said. She shrank down under the bedclothes. Elise stood in the doorway watching.

'Louise eat something and you will feel better,' I implored her. The fear that Louise might be ill was more than I could bear. 'Eat!' I begged her. I fetched some bread and butter. Carefully I put the plate on a tray and laid it on the bed beside the thin shape she made under the blanket. 'Only try,' I said. 'Only eat something Louise.' She could not eat. I felt certain she would be better if she ate the bread and butter. I put squares of it to her dry cracked lips.

'She doesn't want it,' Elise said in her thick voice. She ate the bread and butter herself, sitting on the linoleum with her fat legs wide apart. The sight of her dirty underwear annoyed me.

'Get up!' I shouted at her. I slapped her and she howled.

155

For the rest of the afternoon she whimpered and sniffed. Towards evening I put more bread and butter beside Louise, adding a glass of cold tea. She made no attempt to take either. I thought she was asleep. Later, Elise ate the bread and upset the tea into Louise's blanket.

When Elise was in bed I sat beside Louise listening to her uneasy breathing. The melancholy sound of the wind and a ship's siren, far away, made the night long and lonely. I wondered what I should do.

'Norman is coming,' I whispered. 'Get up and get dressed!' Norman never came during the night. If Louise thought he was coming perhaps she would move about. If she could just be well and busy, even if only in an unhappy way, I felt it would not be so bad. 'Norman's coming!' I said again.

I thought about Elise. Suddenly her breasts had become towers on her childish body. She sat all day, rocking to and fro, playing with stuffed toys and an assortment of rags. She sang to the rags and talked to them. She accepted everything about herself with a mild interest. The day her period started she peered at herself and took the packet of sanitary pads Louise gave her with the same pleasure as if she had been given a present.

In the night I was sorry for Elise.

'Louise! I'm sorry I smacked Elise,' I remembered the quiver of her flesh and the red mark my hand made. 'I'm sorry Louise. I'll be nice to Elise. I'll be kinder. I'm sorry. I'll be different.' Louise did not turn over or wake up. I tried again.

'Louise! Come! Listen to me! I have to speak low so as not to disturb Elise. Listen to me! I want everything to be different. I know we only have a small house and that we are poor. It's all my fault and I'm sorry. I want us to start again. Will you Louise? Louise do you remember when were children together . . .?'

The noise of the wind outside reminded me of the old house. It made the same noise; somewhere a piece of corrugated iron rattled and flapped. Louise once asked me, 'Do you think I'm pretty Jacob?' and she told me she had

156

made me a ring out of her own hair. 'See,' she said then. 'See it is plaited and woven especially for you.'

Louise was not whispering. The only sound in the room was her harsh breathing.

'Louise does it hurt you to breathe? Louise your hands are so cold and yet your head is like fire, shall I fetch a doctor? I could put a cold cloth on your head. Would you like a cold, wet cloth on your head? Please tell me Louise what you would like. Louise be well again. Please.'

They, Tante Rosa and Louise were so strange about doctors. No doctor was sent for when Tante Rosa was dying. Only for the stinking charred remains of the one time Grenadier did a doctor appear to a sign away on paper what had already gone. Perhaps they had promised her that no one, not even a doctor, from outside the house would look upon her pathetic, burned body. Waldemar had been kept hidden. It was clear to me now, remembering his quiet departure, that with a doctor's advice, perhaps only a few little tablets prescribed, he could have had an entirely different life.

Louise must have a docotor. She was ill.

I tried again to rouse her. The night seemed as if it would go on for ever. I sang to Louise.

> 'Come to me, I'm coming to you,
> You must answer me, my angel . . .'

My voice cracked. 'I'll buy you a nice dress tomorrow and one for Elise. I'll start early and sell and sell. No more sitting here and doing nothing. You'll see! Perhaps Norman will come tomorrow. Louise! Shall a fetch a doctor?'

I went to the door. I went back to the bedside. It was cold. I must find a doctor. I went out of the house. The wind still moaned up the hill. The nouses, one above the other crazily piled up the steep street, were dark. Everyone would be asleep in the empty night. I went to knock at the house where Elise spent her days. The old woman there would be sure to know what to do. I knocked on the door and on the window. No light appeared and there was no sound from inside the house. All the time the wind was tearing and sighing, it came crying from the harbour up the narrow street.

Louise might refuse to see a doctor. I went back and closed the door, thankful to be inside the house again. Louise was still asleep.

'Louise don't breathe in that way!' I went to the door again. 'I am just going to look for a doctor.' I closed the door on the blackness. I sat down on the floor beside the door.

'Norman will come tomorrow,' I told her. I kept telling her Norman was coming.

Next morning when I woke up I could hear Elise rustling the bread paper. She was eating the sliced loaf, piece by piece, straight from the wrapping. Beside me, in her cold bed, in the cold little room, Louise still slept. Her eyes were open as though she had looked for me in the lonely hours of the night. She might have called me. I had not heard. She slept even though her eyes were wide open. She did not see. I knew I would never hear her voice again and that there was no expression in her eyes. I sank down and wept.

'I'll come with you on your rounds the next few days,' Norman said. His face was swollen. He cried because of Louise.

'You must draw her close,' he said, 'like this.' In his pocket he had a little card with the dates on it of all the holidays he and Madge had together.

'In our thirty years of marriage,' he said, smiling over the smudged card. 'This is better than a photograph,' he said. 'When I look at this and see the place names and the dates it's just as if we were driving or walking and seeing things together as we once did.' He put the card away.

'Draw her close,' he said.

How could I draw anyone close. I had no one. A whole

lifetime was on the little card Norman had. He kept it in the pocket, I noticed, inside his jacket, just over his heart. I had no list of dates and when I tried to think of the hut and the old house a terrible confusion was all I seemed to have.

I had nothing except Elise.

'Anyways, I'll come with you on your rounds the next few days.' Norman often repeated things more than once. 'Next few days I'll come with you.'

'She will have to come too.'

'Yes, yes of course, Elise,' Norman fussed about and found a piece of old cloth. He gave it to her.

'Dust up the jars and bottles lovey,' he said.

Norman's jacket was shabby in the bright sunshine and the cuffs were frayed. He trimmed them with a pair of nail scissors. We stood together on the neglected verandah of a closed up house waiting for someone to come and open the door.

'Case all ready?' Norman smoothed his jacket. 'Must have put on the wrong coat by mistake,' he smiled, 'doesn't exactly go with the trousers if you see what I mean.' I knew it was the only jacket he had. In comparison my clothes were of good quality and scarcely worn.

I had no money left at all. In spite of Aunt Mitzi's advice, I had wasted it all in selfish foolishness. Aunt Mitzi had shrugged with more than impatience and declared she would have nothing more to do with me.

Uncle Otto and Mitzi, after years of careful investment, were travelling. I received a postcard from Gibraltar. It was a coloured picture of an ape dressed to look like a wealthy tourist.

'Whose photograph?' was written in Mitzi's handwriting on the back. It came two days after the funeral.

I thought I would visit Aunt Heloise. She would be waiting for Louise to come. Aunt Heloise might remember why Madge had come to the house that afternoon. Every day I thought of going to see her but every day, for different reasons, I put off going.

The following Sunday Norman came as usual. He prepared the meal. He said he would teach Elise to make a pudding.

'My wife used to make this,' he said. His wife, Madge, my Madge. My head ached.

Norman asked Elise for a bowl and a wooden spoon. She was pleased and stood close to him, her fat stomach rested on the edge of the table.

'You can break the eggs lovey,' he said. She was completely happy cracking eggs.

'It's called Fluff Pudding,' Norman said. It was just the name Madge would have for a pudding. She would have started making it much too late. Always she began her cooking at the last minute, too late to be ready. Lemons rolled on the table and Norman spilled the flour.

Suddenly he sat down.

'You wouldn't know this,' he said in a broken voice. 'But this was her birthday, it's her birthday today. I've tried and tried,' he said, 'I'm sorry!' and he wept.

I wanted to tell Norman he was an old fool and I wanted to weep too. Madge had loved me not him. Then I had to remember all the dates and places on the dirty worn card. There must have been a lot of time for Madge and Norman when I simply had not existed for Madge. I had not even known when Madge's birthday was. What, I wondered, was so precious and noble about my love in comparison to this kind of devotion.

Elise was still breaking eggs.

'I'm sorry. I must go and see someone,' I told Norman.

'Oh yes of course! Tucker time when you get back.' Norman stood up and pretended to salute, flour dropping from his fingers.

Aunt Heloise was sitting in her dishevelled bed piecing together her coloured bits of cloth. The room was badly lit as there was a closed in verandah where the windows were. It seemed airless too and lined with old ladies, all of them stout and smelling of urine.

'Can you see if this is blue or purple?' Aunt Heloise said to me holding up two fragments of cloth. It was hard to see what they were.

'Aunt Heloise,' I whispered. 'Why did Madge come to the house? Did she tell you why she came?' Urgently I whispered; the nurses were bringing the lunch trays. It was not really visiting time.

'I am going away,' I told the Sister. 'I must see my dear aunt before I go,' I said bowing slightly and I was allowed to stay. Some of my sense of personal charm and privilege returned and I turned back to Aunt Heloise and playfully asked her the same question again.

'She came because, you know dear,' Aunt Heloise lowered her voice drawing me close. 'You know dear! Things are not the same for us now, Rosa you know, never comes now except at night sometimes, you know how it is with Rosa—'

'Aunt Heloise, remember Madge!' I spoke sharply. 'I want to know why Madge came to our house that day. Try to remember, I took Tante Rosa to see the big house where we were all going for a holiday, remember? Madge came and something happened. Tell me please. Try to think. What happened that day.'

Aunt Heloise laughed softly. 'Yes I will tell you,' she said. 'She came because . . .' her voice trembled. 'She came because — I wonder if ziss iss a blue one and if ziss is a purple one?' she pulled at the bits of cloth. I waited anxious and hopeful that she could tell.

'Lunch Aunty!' a cheerful little nurse came with a tray. Aunt Heloise tried to give me the soup.

'Eat,' she said. 'Boys need to eat all the time. Rosa worries if you do not eat.'

It was useless. I went out and drove off in my shabby car. It was fragrant with all the things I had to sell. I owed Norman for my stock.

I seemed to see Aunt Heloise's crumpled face and her watery faded eyes. As I drove, I went on trying to make her speak.

'You know dear . . .' I seemed to hear her voice and I wanted to make her talk.

The scent of the bath salts in the car and my confused thoughts became too much and I longed to rest. It seemed impossible to go back to Norman and Elise. I thought if I went somewhere quietly to sleep perhaps Louise would come or Madge. Louise or Madge.

'You know dear! Things are not the same for us now, Rosa you know, never comes now except at night sometimes. You know how it is with Rosa—.' I was driving the car and listening again to Aunt Heloise, giddy old lady on her pillows.

Perhaps they would come to me at night sometimes. Which one would come?

Madge, Louise. Can a man love two women? Can I love anyone? Does anyone love me? No, it should be, did anyone love me?

So I drove the car.

It was already night. The trembling in my legs frightened me. I drove into the wide asphalt drive of a motel. Red and yellow lights framed the sign and the receptionist was yellow edged with red. I longed for rest and sleep.

'Name?'

'Jacob,' I fumbled for my surname, 'er . . .'

'Address Mr Jacob?'

She handed me a slip of paper.

'Fill out your breakfast chit sir? Tick the boxes.'

Tomato juice orange juice cornflakes eggs bacon chops toast coffee tea milk dancing black and white juice tick cream tick tick tick tick.

She handed me a key.

'Drive on down, first left, first right, green door. Good night sir.'

Smell of pine and the warmth of a closed up room closed up all day clean in the smell of pine comfortable clean and in order in order —

'— Oh there's a telly,' Madge plumping her thick body

162

on the bed, 'I'll try the mattress I'll christen the loo oh all that lovely hot water I'll wash my hair,' Madge laughing, 'Get dressed Jackyboy I'll wash all our clothes Anything in the fridge I'm starving Come to bed Jackyboy Come to bed Don't let's wait for Anything I hope they don't bring the breakfasts too early,' Madge breathing hard —

Louise creeps about the strange arrangement of rooms.

'It's very clean and nice Jacob' her voice is a tiny whisper. 'Explain to Tante Rosa how clean it is here. You will have to show them how the shower works. They are not used to these taps Jacob. Come to bed Jacob. It is all right. It is in order. Come to bed. It is expected of us. You are so tired come and sleep.'

'I didn't know you had the boots!' like the sharp unexpected pain the stab of a big metal needle, my voice in the empty room frightens me. Of course I am alone.

I must remember that.

'Where are your boots Louise!'

I was alone, the sound of my own voice a shock; I took off my clothes and went to the shower. It was a complicated tap. I did not understand it. Scalding water streaked my white skin red. I slipped and fell, my thin ankles ridiculous above my head. My pale elbow, like a clown's, caught in the towel rail. Blood mixing with the hot water and the pain of the scald made me cry out. I struggled out comforting my hurt body with the thick towels.

> *Ach, in den Armen hab ich sie alle verloren,*
> *du nur, du wirst immer wieder geboren:*
> *weil ich niemals dich anhielt, halt ich dich fest.*

'Louise please translate the words for me.'
'But you do not need them translated Jacob.'
'Please please Louise I want to sing them.'
'So, here you are then,

> *All whom I held in my arms did not remain*
> *but you are reborn again and again:*
> *because I never held you, I hold you for ever.'*

163

'You don't love anyone except yourself Jacob. You don't want the words to sing for me Jacob. You want them for someone else.'

'Louise, let's start again from when we were children. Remember Louise when we were children?'

'See Jacob I have written something on this paper for you, it is for you, take it and read it.'

'"You seem to have lost the real meaning of the feeling for compassion." What do you mean, Louise, what does this writing mean. "You disturb all the tired surfaces." Louise what do you mean?'

When I woke up Louise was not there and nothing at all was written.

The plane trees are in pale green leaf and restless outside the windows of the place where Aunt Heloise is but she cannot see them through the frosted glass.

'Aunt Heloise, please tell me why did Madge come to the house?'

'Ah dear Jacob?' She came because — but where was I — you know Dear Jacob, Leopold married with a Jewess so we fled. Rosa, she had to pack everything, books and valuables and we had to take them to Switzerland secretly. I am telling you why and everything why she comes to the house on zat day, but first I am in my prayers. Remember Jacob?

> *Herr, ich glaube,*
> *Herr, ich hoffe,*
> *Herr, von Herzen lieb ich Dich!*

'Remember Jacob? Say your prayer, repeat the prayer Jacob.'

'Yes Aunt Heloise,' just as when I was a boy, I begin,

> *'Lord I believe*
> *Lord I hope*
> *Lord with all my heart, I love you.'*

164

Aunt Heloise nodding and smiling, says;

> *'Sollten alle Menschen lügen*
> *Kannst Du mich doch nicht betrügen!*
> *Nichts ist Dir, O Gott, verborgen,*
> *In den Glauben, in der Hoffnung,*
> *In der Liebe stärke mich!*

Now Jacob?'

> *'Even if all men should lie*
> *You cannot deceive me*
> *Nothing is hidden from you Oh, God.*
> *Your word, I believe without fear,*
> *In belief. In hope. In Love strengthen me.'*

I wait for her,

> *'Herr, ich glaube, Herr ich hoffe ...'*

Aunt Heloise is tired of prayers.

'No one seems to hear them,' she says smiling and nodding. She likes the consulting room and the spinning chair. 'I shall spin a little in ziss chair.' Aunt Heloise is spinning faster and she is Madge slowly stopping and starting the chair in the opposite direction. Madge is laughing spinning laughing higher and higher. I am spinning too. Higher! Falling turning still and falling. The height is tremendous. I am looking down as I fall.

'Oh my God! The pain!' I woke in the quiet room and pressed the wet towels to my thigh and I groaned aloud with the pain.

'You do the next house Jacob,' Norman is out of breath as the road is uphill. 'You knock this time Jacob. Open your case straight away and show the products. Remember what I have told you — "May I rest my case on your table?" You do the next house.'

'Oh I can't do it Norman not in front of you.'

'How the sun shows up shabby things Jacob, look you, at my old coat! It's the only one I have but I pretend you see I pretend.'

We are going to Norman's house together. He has invited me. The manure coloured sadness of the house is hidden in elaborate preparations.

'Here on the television set Jacob are three little gold purses wasted money spilling out of them and here in the kitchen heaps of fantastic shells and these two travelling rugs are to cover it all up. Under these tartan fringes we can hide all the confusion. My wife, Jacob, is not interested in housework. She plays the violin and is interested in other things. She is dead now, Jacob, I don't think I will be able to get over her death ever.'

'Neither can I Norman.' I woke again and pressed the towels to my pain.

'Carbon and its allotropes as crystalline forms graphite and diamond. See Jacob how I have been learning especially to teach you. Coal is mostly amorphous carbon although it contains many complex organic compounds of C with hydrogen, oxygen and nitrogen.' Leopold lets me do anything I like on our walks to the hospital. He strokes me with his lovely fingers. I can't understand his explanations. My feet cool in the water sprinklers. I feel made all over again, like the magpies when they stand under the water jets. Leopold is gentle.

'When I was a young man I will tell you, Jacob, I was sent with two other prisoners to dig graves and the place for the graves was a mass of flowers. While I am digging in the fresh earth, Jacob, I am free, digging graves in freedom with flowers stalks and petals and colours and scents. For the first time in my life I am seeing beauty, simple perfect beauty alive.'

'Why were you a prisoner Leopold?'

'We are all prisoners Jacob and the graves we dig are for ourselves, ultimately, for us. We are all prisoners until we carefully look on the stalks and the petals, Prince of a Fellow! It is not sad, remember it is not sad. Remember Leopold tells you.'

166

I woke shouting, my head and my feet were burning and yet I shivered. I called for them. I could not breathe and pain was all over my body.

XX

Sometimes, on the few occasions when I was at the hut or in the house with Madge, I was irritable and hard to please. It was because, during those times, there was no music and there was nothing to read. In between the love-making there seemed to be absolutely nothing, though we had disturbing and often quarrelsome conversations. I needed something more than love-making and eating. I never spoke of this to Madge.

'Oh the country!' Madge stretched and yawned. 'In the country all there is to do is eat and you know what!' She was always cooking. Wherever she was, she heaped wood into the stove, mixed things in little bowls, prepared dressings for salads and followed the directions on packets of cake mix. She ate up alone or with Norman quite greedily, the two of them enjoyed food, the things she made. We did not have many occasions alone together. I woke in the motel

168

bed recalling the weekend when we had all four been at the hut. Perhaps the place had, at that time, the same effect, that of being spiritually a wilderness, for Louise. Because of her illness then, we had never talked about it. Louise too might have known this same melancholy.

The motel would have the same desolation of being without music and without books. A traveller would need to bring his own poetry to such a place.

'Breakfast!' there was a muffled scream outside. 'Breakfast!' Coming nearer with a noise of badly made keys my room was unlocked from outside. 'Breakfast!'

The bloodstained towel had to be extricated from my deformed hand. The claw-like quality of the hand made this difficult. The part of the towel pressed into my groin was stuck to the painful wound. A woman in a blue overall bent over me. The breakfast tray, tilting, sent a cascade of little brightly coloured cereal packets over the blankets. Surely I had not ordered so many.

'Oh my Gawd!' she said. 'Oh! my Very Gawd! Don't you move!' she said as I tried to get up and apologize.

'Don't you move,' she said and, taking the tray, she left the room at once. From some distant place I heard her screeching.

They could not tell me enough how sorry they were that I had hurt myself in their motel accommodation. Anxious eyes searched my face. Cool hands dressed the wounds. Voices were gentle, even pleading. Perhaps I would let the matter rest.

The manager himself came to show me the shower taps and he demonstrated how easily they could be turned on and off. Would I accept something? A gift, or a holiday in their motel without paying, a week or a fortnight? A month if I wished?

All day I rested there, sipping slowly a golden broth with little dabs of butter melting, spreading in mint flecked rings. My lips hovered over the fragrant surface of this tender nourishment.

'She has cried all the time,' Norman pale and creased with lack of sleep met me at my door. 'She has not stopped her crying,' he said, 'she wanted you to come home.' He seemed to blame himself. 'She has cried and cried, poor little girlie!'

To amuse her he had taken out a box of things put away by Louise. She had an old cabin trunk in our bedroom. In the old house there had been many such trunks, all of them carefully packed with linen and glass and silver. In one of them several bundles of notes had been hidden. My money stored away in a manner preferable to them and burned on the day when I threw the heater and set fire to the room.

'It is vulgar to display one's possessions,' Aunt Heloise said once when, after my marriage, I expressed in a moment of conversation, my amazement that the dinner-table treasures were hidden away instead of being brought out to be used every day. Louise had inherited this habit of keeping things neatly packed, even small presents which she received she put away as if to save them for some future misfortune. Perhaps, I thought, it belonged to the life of the refugee, to be always ready to move on, to be always ready to take flight.

Elise sat with her fat legs wide apart on the cold linoleum. It was irritating and touching that she never seemed to notice that her unwashed underclothes were showing. Her round face was pink and rubbed, smeared, where Norman had tried to wipe it, with dirt and tears.

In the box were a few old photographs. Norman had them all lined up on the mantlepiece. Tante Rosa, the Grenadier in sepia, looked down into the meanness of the little room. Heloise and Rosa photographed in an orchestra of unknown people. All serious, starved looking people, all closely buttoned to their chins with covered buttons and high collars. Aunt Heloise was round like a china doll and dripping with ringlets. No one else had curls. Ignoring Norman and the crying child I searched hungrily along the line of lifeless faces. I had not seen the photographs before though I knew Louise had them. Leopold was there in a fur hat and a travelling cloak with a cape made of fur. Louise in a tiny sailor frock, her feet big in buttoned boots and her legs two stumps in white hand knitted socks. She held in dimpled hands a doll I had never seen. Tante Rosa again, severe and nervous for her photograph. As I peered at her carefully, I saw that behind the severe expression was a shy hopefulness. I remembered the unexpected charming voice and the little impertinent movements she made, tossing her head, when she sang the Brahms folk songs. Songs which suggested love and desire and happiness.

I wanted to tell Norman I was sorry. I could only look along the photographs. Helplessly I looked at them and at Norman.

'Listen!' he said, 'we found a treasure!' He wound up the old gramophone. My new elaborate one had been sold. He put a small record on and, after some scratchy background noises, there came the sound of a piano. Elise listened with pleasure.

'She has heard it already,' Norman explained softly. 'She likes it.'

When I heard the thin, untrained voice singing I did not know who it was. The singer sounded young and shy and it was clear that English was not her accustomed language. Delight spread over Norman's face; he watched me as I listened.

'The record's old,' he whispered, 'but the voice is very young and very beautiful.'

As I listened the vine leaves fresh and young and green bursting from the gnarled wood seemed to caress my face.

> *Come, down, O love divine*
> *Seek thou this soul of mine*
> *And visit it with thine own ardour glowing;*
> *O comforter, draw near,*
> *Within my heart appear*
> *And kindle it, thy holy flame bestowing.*

I remembered my mother's voice then; her cradle songs and

the singing games which she sang in a sweet voice faltering and flat, clearing her throat, starting and stopping, and then starting again to avoid a note which was too high. She sang while she cleaned the house. No one took any notice of her singing. No one listened to her songs or remarked on her voice except sometimes my father would ask her to try to remember the words and the music of a certain song and she would shake her head and run laughing into the vineyard. That was a long time ago.

'She could have been a great singer,' Norman nodded his head wisely.

'But she wasn't.' I took off the record before it was finished. I stopped the thin schoolgirl voice. She must have learned the English words on purpose to sing the hymn. It was too late to wish I had known my mother more. There was no one to turn back to now; no one to tell things to.

Listening to my mother's voice I thought of all the houses, the dark half-remembered rooms of my childhood and the hall and the stairs and the scrubbed kitchen of the house where I lived for so many years. I thought of the large house with the discreet consulting room and the comfortable spacious rooms on the upper floors. I had hoped to put people into layers, literally in layers, in the big house, safely on my own terms. I had actually thought it would be possible to put people neatly into places convenient to me.

'Take her out,' I said to Norman. I wanted to be alone to tear up the old photographs, to break the record. I wanted to destroy and spoil but not in front of Norman.

'But there is our work,' Norman said gently. 'Jacob we have to go out to our customers. Come!' he said. 'Time is money! Get ready! I'll meet you when we've both had time to freshen up.' I knew he was smiling his kind, sad smile even though I could not look at him.

'What about her?' I was ashamed of the tone of my voice but I did not change it. 'What about her!'

'Bring her of course,' he said. 'Lovey,' he said to Elise, 'wash your face, lovey, and put on a nice clean frock. You can come out with Daddy and Nunky Norman. You can come out and dust up the jars and bottles. I'll bring out a nice rag. Nunky'll bring a lovely rag. There's a good girl. Just you stop your crying now.'

Hanging round the bedroom were our clothes; there was no cupboard. Louise's clothes were still there on hangers dangling on nails. Elise undressed herself and chose one of Louise's dresses. I snatched it from her. She laughed and chattered about the dresses choosing another one which belonged to Louise.

'Be quiet! No, not that one!' I roared at her. My thigh ached and my movements were slow. She stood, suddenly silent, with her back to me, her head bent forward waiting for me to button her frock. Impatiently I pulled the garment across her broad, pink, spotty back. I could not make the buttonhole meet the button.

'Haven't you got something else to put on?' I shouted. She pulled out her pyjamas.

'No they won't do!' I shook her after I had managed to fasten one of the buttons. She went slowly to the car and sliding into the back seat she sat with her head bent down. On all sides of her were the fragrant cartons of perfumes, lipsticks, shampoos, spices, cleaning materials and bathsalts.

Though I tried to think of going to Norman, to set off with him to try to sell the products, I was obsessed with wanting to know why Madge had gone to the house that afternoon. She knew I was going to tell them about the house and the proposed holiday. Had she later changed her mind about it?

'Try and get them to agree,' she said. I seemed to hear her voice again and to feel her firm flesh between my fingers. I pinched her for fun that day. I felt her warm softness between my thighs too; it was with an ache of loneliness I thought of her now.

She would never have received the letter I wrote that afternoon when I had taken Tante Rosa to see the house.

As I drove to Norman's house the thought occurred to

me that the letter will have been delivered to his house and that he will have received it. All the time he will have known what I wrote on that day.

> *. . . I can't wait Dearest to have you there all night.*

How could he have seen my letter and continued to come and help me. As I drove I pondered on his noble character and on his kindness. The afternoon, all those years ago, seemed to be yesterday. I never posted the letter. I pushed it into my pocket that afternoon. I never saw it again. Now, I understood.

Louise was the one who saw the letter. She will have seen, *I can't wait Dearest to have you there all night.* She will have known the words were not for her.

Blood red flowers on white walls, her red lips on his pallid skin, memories mingled with the fragrance of fresh cut grass along the streets of my selling area. Red flowers, the poinsettias brilliant on the white walls reminding of the horrible secret love-making in the top room in that house. I stopped the car. I wanted to vomit but we were by a bus stop and little girls were standing there waiting, like flowers, to be picked. A blind man was being helped across the road by his friend, another blind man. I often saw the little girls waiting. I wondered what the two men did, whether they spent the whole day together, what their work was and how they lived. I did not think of them or of the little girls for long; mostly I thought about myself.

Elise sang in the back of the car, no real words just a monotonous singing. Years ago Waldemar's rat sang softly in its cage, buried in shredded newspaper. Elise played with the little bottles of instant flavouring, raspberry, vanilla, almond, peppermint, banana, strawberry and lemon. She arranged them along the seat talking to the brightly coloured essences.

It was no use to go back to see Aunt Heloise.

'We are not ourself today,' the Sister was blue and white

and kind. 'We are not ourself. We are thinking it is quite in order to go out to the shops in our nighty! Come another day. Perhaps we shall be better on another day.' A smile of white teeth. 'Aunty is a naughty girl today.'

I turned off the road which led to Norman's house. Perhaps he was standing smiling and waiting in the middle of his manure coloured carpet. I drove slowly along the road which had once been the edge of a swamp where pale ghost trees without heads implored, with their dead branches, for some sort of life. Where there had once been oozing mud and rubbish was now all smoothed over with grass. A golf course was there and a children's playground. There was an ornamental lake with a little bridge and there were flowers and young trees, saplings, tied firmly to posts and labelled. Perhaps the rubbish in a person's life could be pushed somewhere beneath a smooth skin. Perhaps a shining and elastic skin could grow and, in place of a decrepit human being, there could be something radiant and glowing.

I looked on the soft grass and the flowers as if for the first time, remembering the desolate place it had once been.

'A Prince of a Park,' Leopold might have said if he had seen it, scorning it yet liking it, approving at the same time.

'A Prince of a Fellow,' he called me. I should be a prince, I thought, instead of the thing I had become.

I would go on. The avenue of trees was the same. I would go on and visit Waldemar.

Waldemar has passed into a different world where it might not be possible to reach him. I had never reached him. From that world, for him, there was no return.

'Sit here in the car till I come back,' I told Elise. 'It's nice here under the trees. Stay here till I come,' I told her.

Whatever world Waldemar was in I thought I would try to see him.

XXI

The great staircase and the green and blue and white and gold entrance hall were quite unchanged. The same ferns leaned and drooped from the same cauldrons of polished brass. The nun's robes were white and solid like the marble of the steps.

Though the lift was full of visitors I allowed myself to be sucked across the mosaic of the hall and into the small over-crowded space.

Doors were swiftly and smoothly unlocked and locked as the people flocked through. I went by the cots of sleeping children and through the women's section to the place where I might find Waldemar. Among all the fair and tousled heads, where bodies and minds jostled in that crowded place, I was unable to see him. It was hard to distinguish where one man ended and another began. Faces, one after another, loomed in front of me as I peered to find the one I wanted. Eyes were as if without sight. No one recognized anyone. There was a sweetness as of fruit confined in boxes and of sugar sticks forgotten and soft in their wrappings. There was a smell of breath and sweat and unwashed clothes, even though the clothes were washed all the time.

I could not find Waldemar.

I walked down the wide curving marble stairs.

'Why are these here?' I asked Leopold once.

'What do you mean?'

'Well, I mean these marble steps, shouldn't they be in a palace?'

'They are the work of craftsmen,' Leopold said. 'You are right. On the other hand, it is right that there is something extravagant and beautiful for the people in here.'

It was clear that a great deal of washing was done. In between the buildings, in closed in yards, were heavy lines of washing. Sheets, towels, nightshirts, all kinds of clothing, grey from repeated washings, hung dripping, motionless, on the low lines. At the back of the hospital there were sheds and vegetable gardens and a poultry yard. I lingered near the noisy ducks and hens. They had a life all of their own. They were tremendously occupied with this life.

In front of the hospital were flower gardens and a grassy parkland. The grass, freshly cut, smelled sweet. Perhaps Waldemar would be out there somewhere in the park, in the shadow of the high wall. I wanted to find him, to ask him my question. He would understand. Years ago I had asked him.

'Waldemar, unlock the bolt for me.' He was asleep then and I had to shake his bulky body and repeat my request till he understood.

I could not stand the sight of all the visitors in the grounds. I must, by some chance, have come on an open day of some sort. Crowds of people in holiday clothes, men in shorts and open shirts and girls in the harsh yellows and reds of cheap synthetic materials, strolled about the gardens as if they were visiting a zoo. Their faces were without expression

177

and I experienced the same sadness and melancholy which came over me so often when I was out trying to sell the cosmetics and the spices which no one seemed to want. These same people too were in the beach cafes where I sometimes sat. For some reason their lives seemed apparently empty and aimless.

I turned my face away not wanting to reflect the lack of expression. Madge told me more than once that I was beautiful.

I heard singing from the open windows of the women's hall. So they sang still as they used to sing with Leopold. It was a dreary noise, out of tune, flat and dragging. Words and tunes which, having no meaning for the singers, seemed aimless.

I tried to remember Mozart. I sang to myself beneath the window. Though the sounds of the music poured through my head no sound came from my lips and I could remember only one line from the Requiem.

And every secret sin arraign
Till nothing unavenged remain.

It seemed to have no meaning and yet once I thought it must be profound and wise. When Louise taught me the working of a sum, 'Just tell the answer,' I said to her with feelings of impatience, 'don't bother to tell me how to do it.'

The words from the Requiem I lovingly learned by heart. Now I wanted explanations, words to explain other words and to explain the thoughts and feelings in the music. And I wanted an explanation, a reason to explain why Madge had come to the house that day.

I wanted to know, perhaps for the first time in my life, why I was alive at all. And, whatever was I going to do next.

The singing from above stopped and an elderly voice sang alone. She was singing to herself, for in this place no one listened. People made noises, they spoke and sang, they ate and drank and slept and held on to life greedily. Was every person really doing all these things only for himself? I stopped still in among the wooden tubs of lemon trees which were like lanterns scattered along the side of the building.

> '*My soul is thirsting for God, the God of my life,*'

she sang.

> '*Like the deer that yearns for running streams*
> *My soul is thirsting for the Lord.*
> *When shall I see Him face to face?*'

The lonely singing was like the thin, sad voice of my mother on the record, except that this singer was an old woman and not a young girl.

Perhaps the terror and failure of my life could, in some way, be smoothed over like the swamp had been levelled and drained and combed and planted. Perhaps a fine, smooth skin could cover the misery I had now. Perhaps I could start again with all the experience packed under the skin.

I stepped out from the shadow of the wall into the sunshine of the park. The well-kept lawns beckoned but they reminded too of the empty streets and the closed houses of my selling area. I had no energy to set off. Slowly I went over to the place where Elise was sitting in the car waiting. There was a crowd of people round the car. I felt afraid and wondered what they were doing here. I hurried across the grass. It was not possible to know which people were visitors and which were patients.

'You hev ziss end you hev ziss,' I heard Elise, 'end you have ziss, her lisping soft voice went on and on. I made my way through the crowd and found her giving away the products. The only things we had to live on.

'You hev ziss,' she said smiling fondly at an old woman and giving her a plastic urn of bath crystals. 'You hev ziss,' an old man held out his hand for a tin of ointment. In the other hand he had a bar of washing soap. Everyone had something from my boxes. I could see that nothing would be left.

My relief was like the carefree rolling over and over down grassy slopes and like that moment of jumping into the silky brown water of the river. Childhood pleasures long forgotten but belonging with the happiness of rushing from the dark shed, where the barrels were made, into the sunny paths between the vines.

Tears of relief filled my eyes as I saw her fat hands handling packages and containers. The sun light on her fair head brought out the gold in her hair.

And then I saw Waldemar. He was standing at the edge of the little crowd. He was big and fat and he was smiling. Someone passed a little jar to him. It looked like a nutmeg sprinkler. He took it and held it to his ear and looked all round the crowd before he sprinkled it on his pale hair. I went over to him.

'Waldemar!'

He quickly closed his two fists together making his two hands into large white balls. The nutmeg shaker had disappeared.

'Which hend you hev?' he asked, moving the great white fists up and down in front of me. His breath was heavy with sugar and milk and biscuits and chocolate. 'Which hend you hev?' Laughter wheezed up out of his huge body. I did not notice the crowd. Would Waldemar recognize me?

'I'm not playing that,' Elise pushed through the crowd her plump body planted in front of Waldemar, she laughed, 'I'm not playing!'

The people were exchanging packets and sniffing and tasting each other's gifts. They were smiling, well pleased with all the things.

'Which hend you hev?' Waldemar did not give up. I stared at him waiting to see if he could know me.

I took Elise by the hand and drew her to Waldemar and pushed her hand into the big loose fist.

'Which hend you hev?'

I took his other hand and somewhere on the grass we left the nutmeg sprinkler.

XXII

'That's a lovely sound, a happy duck quacking because she's found something to eat. Just listen to that duck!' Norman stands near the fence of the poultry yard listening and smiling. And then we walk on. 'No tah!' he says, 'I won't have anything, I'm just over my dinner. I was just passing so I thought I'd drop by.'

Norman stops by on Sundays, he does not stay long. He is always just passing. Sundays I have a half day off work. The patients' lunches are served early on Sundays because of visitors.

'How's things?' Norman asks; we leave the poultry yard and walk together to find an unoccupied bench in the gardens.

'Time goes that quick,' he says, sitting down, 'here today and gone tomorrow. My very word, this sun's nice on my back!'

Already he is looking older, sunburned still because

his work takes him out of doors, but older all the same.

'Yes time does certainly go,' I say, 'I've been here four weeks now. Here,' I say, 'here's some of the money I owe you. Go on take it! I'm going to pay it all back, every cent of it.'

'Well now, if you're sure,' he says, 'there's no rush, you know, I mean you can pay later,' embarrassed, he takes the little envelope from me and puts it carefully into his inside pocket.

'How's things then?' he often repeats himself. We sit and stare at patients and their visitors. I felt relieved that Norman will not stay long because, though I appreciate his coming, I find him incredibly boring. He is not a companion I would choose. 'How's things?' he asks again. It occurs to me that he could find me dull.

The hospital park is ringed with trees, Norfolk Island pines, kurrajong trees, jacarandas and flame trees. Nearby under some magnolias, a mother magpie puts up with the endless wailing of her overgrown baby bird. The baby is an idiot bird.

'Some mothers do have 'em,' Norman always makes the same remark.

I'd like to tell Norman that suddenly now in these last few weeks everything seems clear to me, that it's like the short and splendid relief when severe pain has responded to treatment. Now, even the lives of magpies seem full of meaning.

'You know Norman,' I say, 'everything is outlined clearly and yet polished and softened in these first quiet days without suffering.'

'Is that so!' he says. I am not sure that he understands. 'Is that so!' he repeats himself and smooths his thin white, hair with the clean palms of his hands. 'Is that so!'

Elise comes across the grass.

'And how's our little girl then? How's our girlie today?' He gets up and gives Elise a kiss. She is neat in her uniform.

'My very word!' he says to her, 'that's a nice dress!'

'It's not a dress,' she says, 'it's my uniform.'

'It's a uniform,' I explain to Norman. 'It was cut out and made especially for her, made to measure in the sewing-room here. It only took a day to make.'

'Made to measure! That's nice!' Norman says. 'And are you still carrying the trays to the patients?' he asks her. 'I hope you are, in that dress, I mean uniform, you must look real good carrying the trays.'

'We have traycloths,' she says, 'made of paper, lacy paper.'

'Do you now, well I never, lacy paper, that's nice. Very nice.'

My hands are all black doing vegetables,' Elise holds them out for Norman to see. 'Onions and beetroot!'

'Are they now,' he says. 'Get a lemon, lovey, and rub the juice into your hands. Clean 'em like magic! My wife always whitened her hands with a lemon.' Norman smiles at Elise. She has to go to spread bread and butter for all those trays.

'Have you got a kiss for me then lovey?' She kisses Norman and skips off fat and heavy across the lawns. 'I'm saving up to buy a little Daisy dog,' she calls back.

'It was a lucky thing there being two vacancies when we turned up,' I say to Norman and he agrees.

'As long as the work suits,' he says. 'They don't work you too hard I hope. All that cleaning!'

'Not at all,' I say, 'I'm fortunate to work here. For the first time in my life Norman, I hope you won't mind my going on about this, but it's the first time in my life I am not living on or through somebody else. It's cleaning up after people, but it's work I can do and it is necessary work and that makes all the difference.'

'Too right it does,' he says.

'This place,' I tell him, 'perhaps I've said this before, when you came before, this place is full of people. For a good many of them this is the only kind of life they can have. The only thing that can be done for them is to keep them clean and comfortable.'

Norman nods his head, he encourages me to speak.

'I want you to know, Norman,' I say, 'I could never ever have been what Leopold said I was. He used to call me a prince of the cello. Now I realise that he did not really believe that himself. I am glad I do realise it in time.'

'What d'you mean, "in time"?'

'Well Norman,' I say, 'what would have happened to me if I'd gone on thinking I was what they all made me out to be?'

'I get you,' he says, 'all the same you could play and you could sing. My wife said so and she would not be wrong.'

'Yes, yes, but not like Leopold made me think I could.'

Norman coughs politely.

'I mean there's Waldemar too,' I say. 'You won't see him today, he's working today. He's busy in there. He's the shave orderly. You know what that is? I mean what could be closer to human beings than that! All day he's bent over some man or other, really close to him, talking to him, soaping him and shaving him, then he pats him dry and tells him he'll shave him again tomorrow. Sometimes there's a woman, maybe, needs her head shaved — well, he does that too. I mean, if you think about it, and I have been thinking a lot lately, if you think about it, it was really fear of medicine and fear of being poor that prevented Waldemar from having any kind of life. And now, though he's in here, he's closer to life than a great many people. They kept Waldemar a prisoner so that they could keep me . . . '

'Steady now!' Norman gives his little smile.

'Well it's true and even worse,' I hear my voice, in spite of myself, rising, 'because of their fear and what they did he took her life. Norman!'

'Steady. Steady now!'

'Norman!' I lean towards him. 'You won't mind my asking this, I hope you won't mind my asking, I've asked you before I know, but do you know why Madge came to the house that afternoon?'

Norman looks at me without speaking. His eyes are looking steadily at me.

'My wife,' he says, 'my wife always had a good reason for anything she did.'